Letting Go

A figure was silhouetted in the light of the doorway and Phoebe sensed instantly that it was Griffin. His long legs, strong frame, and proud stance were familiar to her by now. He walked slowly over to her and leaned next to her on the wall, their shoulders touching.

"What a night," Griffin said, looking up at the sky.

Phoebe looked down at the ground. Griffin knew Brad was away in Princeton and wouldn't be back until tomorrow. She closed her eyes and bit her bottom lip.

Finally Griffin spoke. "Maybe you and I should just go out by ourselves."

Phoebe was unable to answer for a moment. Going out alone with Griffin was what she wanted to do more than anything in the world. And yet, she knew she shouldn't. Somehow, that would be cheating on Brad. She knew she would be letting herself go too far.

Books from Scholastic
in the **Couples** series:

COUPLES

CHANGE OF HEARTS

By Linda A. Cooney

SCHOLASTIC INC.
New York Toronto London Auckland Sydney

ISBN 0-590-33390-9

12 11 10 9 8 7 6 5 4   6 7 8 9/8 0/9

Printed in the U.S.A.   06

CHANGE OF HEARTS

Chapter 1

Phoebe Hall felt like she was going to explode. Until a few weeks ago everything had been fine. She had been her normal, dependable, on-top-of-things self. But lately Phoebe had started getting this strange sensation inside. It felt like she was a bottle of soda pop — the kind that her little brother Shawn shook up with his thumb held over the top, all carbonated, fizzy, and about to burst. And the worst part of it was that Phoebe couldn't figure out why the feeling came or how to make it go away.

Like last period in science class. She had been thinking about her boyfriend, Brad, when she started getting the feeling again. Of course Mr. Baylor had picked that moment to call on her.

"Phoebe Hall. Are you there, Phoebe Hall? This is your teacher calling. This is school. Do you remember school?"

Phoebe shuddered as she recalled how Mr.

Baylor had put his hand on her thick red braid of hair and given it a slight tug.

"Oh," she had called out, and then everybody in class had laughed.

"Glad to see you're back," Mr. Baylor had said loudly. "For a minute there it looked like the Twilight Zone."

Phoebe hadn't known what to say then. She had felt herself blushing, her pale skin turning as red as her hair, and her stomach flip-flopping like a pancake on a grill.

Maybe she was making too big a deal out of it. After all, lots of kids spaced out in class, especially nerdy Mr. Baylor's class. But not Phoebe. Phoebe was usually interested and attentive. At least Brad hadn't been there to see.

When she'd tried before to explain the feeling to Brad he'd suggested that the problem was junioritus. Phoebe had never heard of junioritus. Senioritus maybe, but Brad was a senior and he seemed to be just fine, as always. In the two years they'd gone together Phoebe had never known Brad to forget his locker combination, or start crying at an episode of *Love Boat*, or do something dumb like back into another car. He never seemed to have these moments of panic like the ones she had been feeling lately. He never got ruffled, flustered, spaced out, or confused. But then Brad was student body president and Phoebe was . . . well, just Phoebe.

Phoebe stopped and sat down on one of the benches that dotted the quad. It was almost noon and she was supposed to wait for Brad. For the first time she noticed what a beautiful, clean,

2

sparkling day it had become. Fall was in the air, but the sun was bright, the sky blue as a robin's egg, and the dew on the grass was almost gone. It was one of those days that made you want to take ten deep breaths in a row. Phoebe wondered if maybe that might help calm her down .

She took three or four breaths. It helped a little, but there was still something wrong and it made Phoebe feel nervous. Mostly because she couldn't figure out what it was. She was doing well in school. She was an important member of an important crowd at the best public high school in the Washington D.C. area. She and Brad were getting along fine.

Where was Brad, anyway? It wasn't like him to be late. He was probably at another meeting. Maybe some other members of the crowd would show up first. They met every day at their reserved spot. Phoebe thought their spot was the prettiest corner of the quad. Of course it was unofficial — territorial rights over three wooden benches and the grass under three fading cherry trees. Still, it was theirs and the other kids at Kennedy knew not to invade it.

Phoebe decided she needed a better view. She stood on one of the benches to get a clearer look across the quad. Being only five feet two had taught her not to hesitate when it came to climbing and standing on things. Phoebe could see clear over to the football field. Kennedy was spread out and flat, surrounding the quad like the legs of an octopus. The only sight that broke the flat, modern skyline was the steeple of the old chapel, the small colonial building now used as a little theater. Phoebe grabbed a cherry branch to help her balance and a handful of pink flowers came off in her hand.

"Don't jump! It's not that bad!" A playful voice pierced the general din of the quad. Phoebe looked down and saw the top of Laurie Bennington's hennaed head. It was a strange color — like berries mixed with coffee grounds.

"Hi, Laurie. I wasn't going to jump," Phoebe assured her, managing to laugh. Both girls sat down on the bench.

"Oo, great shirt. I love it," Laurie cooed, admiring Phoebe's old blue cub scout shirt.

"Thanks." Phoebe smoothed her soft cotton sleeve. The shirt was typical of her fashion sense, offbeat, boyish, and funky. Phoebe did find it funny that Laurie, who dressed like she was on the cover of *Vogue,* would really admire a boy's shirt that was covered with insignias and merit badges. "Where is everybody?" Phoebe asked.

"Well," began Laurie with a deep breath. Phoebe smiled and shoved her hands into one of the many pairs of pockets on her blue jeans. Laurie had moved to Rose Hill that summer. This was her first semester at Kennedy. But she had quickly gotten into Phoebe's crowd and seemed to know more about what was going on in school than kids who'd been there since tenth grade. She had even managed to make herself social activities director, an almost unheard-of achievement for someone so new.

"I just came from the meeting to plan the Follies — you know, the talent show that Woody is directing. There's tons of kids there just dying

4

to go down in Kennedy history for their great theatrical talents." Laurie paused for air and re-arranged her wide-necked sweater dress so that one shoulder was exposed. She had one of the all-time great bodies.

The Follies! Another thing Phoebe had completely forgotten. Woody had asked her to come to the meeting to audition. Phoebe loved to sing and had almost always been in choir. But you couldn't exactly sing the *Messiah* for a talent show.

"You should try out!" Laurie bubbled as if she read Phoebe's mind. "You are such a good singer. I'll never forget that number you and Woody sang at my party."

Laurie had thrown a getting-to-know-everybody party as soon as she moved to Rose Hill and had managed to get most of the crowd to show up. Even though nobody knew her very well, they found it hard to resist her energy, style, and persistence.

Laurie pushed her short hair out of her eyes and continued with a smile, "That song was so hot. You have a super voice."

"Thanks." Phoebe smiled and looked down at the ground. She never knew how to react to compliments.

"Anyway," Laurie went on, "I saw Sasha in the theater. She's writing a story about the Follies tryouts for the newspaper and, of course, Woody's there too. As for the other kids, well, I have no idea where your boyfriend is, but I know for a fact that Chris and Ted are up on the third floor taking a romantic lunch break." With a sly

5

look and a cock of her head Laurie implied that Phoebe's best friend, Chris, and her boyfriend were off smooching in the hallway. Phoebe knew Laurie was probably right.

"Of course there is other news." Laurie paused and moved in closer. "I'm going to be doing an activities update on the radio station. The student council thought it would be a good idea, and since I'm activities officer, I get to join hunky Peter Lacey and be on Kennedy radio, too." Laurie practically licked her lips when she mentioned Peter's name.

Phoebe wondered if Laurie knew how many girls had made plays for Peter and failed. Peter was one of the most popular members of the crowd. He didn't make the usual lunchtime scene in the quad because he was too busy doing his own noontime show over the school radio station WKND, but that didn't stop him from being someone in demand. Peter was known for being a great DJ, a cool dresser, and heartbreak for about a million different girls. Even gorgeous Laurie would have her work cut out for her if she was going to go after Peter.

"That sounds great," Phoebe finally said. She was beginning to get really hungry and took her container of yogurt out of her book bag.

"Is that all you're eating for lunch? No wonder you have such a great figure," Laurie cooed sweetly.

Phoebe giggled. She didn't know what to say. She knew Laurie was flattering her again.

"Well, I'm on my way over to the radio station," Laurie announced. "Look out, Peter

6

Lacey!" She rubbed her manicured hands together with obvious relish. "I'm going to see if he needs a ride to the football game at Leesberg today," she winked. "Phoebe, do you want a ride? There's plenty of room."

"Gee," Phoebe stalled. She had forgotten about the football game too. "Can I let you know later?"

"Sure. But you have to ride with me if you go. I made Chris promise to ride with me too," said Laurie, flashing a perfect smile. "Just meet me at my car by ten after if you decide to come."

"Great. And good luck at the radio station," Phoebe said.

"Oh, sure" — Laurie breathed deeply — "hopefully I won't need it."

And with that she turned and marched off confidently, causing a freshman boy to just about drop his notebook as she sauntered by. Phoebe wondered if she would ever have the nerve to act like that.

Phoebe scanned the crowded quad once more. Brad was still nowhere in sight. She got up from the bench and wandered over to the little theater. Not that he woud be there. Phoebe couldn't imagine anything less Brad-like than singing or dancing in front of the whole school. Still Phoebe was curious to see what Woody was planning.

As she neared the old steps to the Little Theater, Phoebe could hear snatches of Woody's familiar voice. Just hearing it made her want to giggle. She could see Woody's tall, expressive body gesturing madly, his curly dark hair falling over his thick eyebrows and his mouth moving a mile a minute. She and Woody had been friends since the sixth grade and as far as Phoebe was concerned there was nobody else quite like him.

Carefully, Phoebe pulled the heavy old wooden door open a crack and peeked in. About a dozen kids were spread out in the first few rows of the theater, all concentrating on ways to make this year's Follies the best ever. Sasha was down front scribbling madly, taking down the info for the school paper, and Woody was being his clownish, entertaining self.

"I don't care if you want to break dance while balancing a boiled ham on your nose," Woody sputtered, "singers, dancers, jugglers, actors; hey, you name it, if it's good it goes in the show. After all, this is your chance to expose yourselves to Kennedy," Woody joked as he mimed opening an imaginary raincoat in a parody of a flasher. Phoebe had to laugh. She started to back out the door when Woody caught her.

"Phoeberooni!" he yelled, "I see you hiding there. You get in here with all of us crazy bums!" Everybody turned to look at Phoebe. Sasha gave a quick wave.

"I haven't forgotten those great Fleetwood Mac duets we used to do in junior high," Woody went on. "Come make a fool out of yourself like the rest of us!"

"That's what I'm afraid of," Phoebe bantered. Woody gave her a pleading look. The warmth in Woody's eyes reminded Phoebe that he had always adored her. Though she loved him dearly as a friend, she didn't return his romantic longings. Luckily, Woody was not the type to ever

8

do anything about his feelings, and their friendship continued.

"I've got to go back out and wait for Brad. I'm sure the show will go on without me."

"All right. But just remember, auditions are going to be today, right here, after school. Phoeberooni is not only welcome, but will be sorely missed if she lets her old friend Woody down." He had his hand over his heart in a melodramatic gesture.

"Right, Woody." Phoebe shook her head and walked out. Woody was sweet, but sometimes a little crazy. Phoebe couldn't be in the show. It would be nice, but she was having enough trouble trying to stay sane these days.

Phoebe sighed. Sometimes she worried that she never did anything important. Her friends all did things to make themselves stand out. Sasha wrote for the paper; Peter worked for the radio station; Chris was head of the honor society; Ted played football; Brad ran the student government. What did she do that was special? Not much. Just spaced out in Mr. Baylor's class.

"Phoebe, hey Phoebe!"

Phoebe looked up. Brad was running towards her, tall and so handsome, with a stack of books under his right arm and his left hand waving to get her attention. His brown hair was still half wet from PE, and his face was open and bright. He was wearing tan slacks, a yellow oxford cloth shirt, and the navy sweater vest Phoebe's mom had knit for him last Christmas. When he pulled Phoebe forward to kiss her he smelled soapy and clean.

9

"I'm sorry Pheeb. I had to call home and see if I got anything from Princeton. This clown in front of me took forever on the phone."

Of all the colleges that were interested in Brad, he had his heart set on Princeton. Any day he was expecting a letter telling him the date for his personal interview.

"Did you hear anything?"

"Nah. Not yet. It's driving me crazy." Brad paused to catch his breath and leaned one leg up on a bench. "Oh, Mom talked to my uncle Jake — you know, the doctor who lives near Princeton — anyway, Uncle Jake says you and I can stay at his house when we go up for the interview. He has a friend who did his premed at Princeton, and Uncle Jake says we can all get together."

"Brad, are you sure that your uncle wants to put me up, too? I mean I don't have to go."

"He wants to meet you. And I really want you there with me. Hey, maybe you'll take one look at Princeton and decide to go there, too. Wouldn't that be great?"

Phoebe tried to agree, but she just didn't want to think about college. It was easy for Brad. He knew he wanted to be a doctor and he was going to be one. Phoebe had no idea what she wanted to do. She only knew that when she thought about it, that soda pop feeling usually came back.

Brad seemed to sense that she was troubled about something. "You okay? Don't worry. If Princeton doesn't accept me I won't fall apart or anything." Brad gently put his arm around her

10

and she hid her neck between his chin and his shoulder.

"You'll get in, I'm sure," Phoebe whispered.

"Oh, Pheeb, before I forget" — Brad turned away to grab one of his notebooks. He pulled out a paper scribbled with notes — "they asked me to head the senior planning committee. Do you think you could type these up for me? I don't know how I'm ever going to get all this done."

"Sure," Phoebe said automatically. She looked over the paper. By this time she could make out even the messiest of Brad's notes. Since her parents had a computer that could do word processing, Phoebe had gotten into the habit of typing and printing things for his many meetings. But lately just looking at Brad's notes had made her start to churn inside.

"Thanks. I don't know what I'd do without you. Hey, where is everybody?" Brad asked, finally looking around.

"What?" Phoebe was not listening. She was trying to figure out why just looking at a sheet of paper made her so upset.

"Where's the gang?"

"Woody and Sasha are at the meeting to plan the Follies — you know, the talent show. Um, today Peter does his radio show, and Laurie went to talk to him. I don't know about Chris and Ted."

"Ted's got a game today after school. Against Leesberg Military."

Phoebe nodded dully. Kennedy only played Leesburg Military once a season, and even then it was only a practice game. But somehow over the years a huge rivalry had developed over that one game. Phoebe knew that lots of kids were talking about whether the Kennedy team could finally beat the cadets.

"Brad, are you going to the game?" Phoebe asked.

"Can't. I have a meeting."

Phoebe knew that Brad would have a meeting. Every group at school wanted his advice and leadership, and he would never dream of turning any of them down.

"Brad?"

"Hmm." He looked at her and smiled sweetly.

"I was thinking maybe I should try out for the Follies. Woody wants me to . . ."

"I bet Woody wants you," Brad teased.

Not this again, thought Phoebe. Brad always joked about Woody, but Phoebe knew deep down it really bothered him. Brad's jealousy was absurd because Phoebe found Woody about as sexy as rolled oats. "You know what I mean. Anyway, I thought I might try out."

"Are you serious? Remember how dumb that show was last year?"

Phoebe shrugged. "Maybe this year it will be a lot better. Woody wants me to sing."

"Come on, Pheeb. The reason Woody wants you in that silly show is because he has the hots for you. He always has and he always will. . . ."

"I know Woody likes me, but he'd never do anything about it. I can't believe you'd be jealous of Woody."

"I'm not jealous of Woody. That show is just

12

a waste of time. If you really want to go make a fool of yourself in front of everybody . . . go ahead."

Phoebe wasn't sure what she wanted to do. It certainly wasn't worth fighting over. She put her face in her hands and pressed on her temples. Brad was probably right. The Follies were kind of dumb.

"Hey," he whispered, tenderly brushing a strand of hair away from her face, "I love you."

Phoebe looked at his eyes and took his hand in hers. She held it tight, for a moment clenching his fingers as hard as she could. She was fizzy inside again. The more she looked into Brad's face the stronger and more confusing the sensation seemed. With a very deep breath Phoebe struggled to ignore her feelings and pretend that everything was just fine.

Chapter 2

"Ted, somebody's coming!" Chris whispered fiercely as she halfheartedly pushed her boyfriend away. She managed to get a few inches between her shoulder and his, but Ted's forearm was still anchored tightly around her back. They were huddled together in a small nook at the end of the third floor hall. Frozen and silent, they waited for the sound of a locker door banging shut and the echo of clunky footsteps to fade down the other end of the hall. Then they both started to laugh.

"Everybody's probably wondering where we are," Chris said as she regained control and smoothed her long blond hair.

"Let them wonder," Ted said in a low voice. He took her hand from her hair and intertwined her fingers with his. Slowly and gently he kissed her again.

This time Chris broke away, but not until

after she'd thoroughly enjoyed the kiss. She primly retucked her plaid blouse into the waistband of her gathered corduroy skirt.

"Ted, we're not supposed to be here during lunch. We're acting like we're in junior high."

"Oh, yeah? Who did you do this with in junior high?"

Chris stifled a laugh and gave him a mock dirty look. "Let's go."

"Aw, come on," Ted said with an innocent smile that usually made her give in. "All right," he said when he saw that this time, she was determined. "But first tell me, are you coming to my game this afternoon or not?"

"I told you. It depends," Chris answered seriously.

She started ahead of him down the hallway. She was already embarrassed for letting Ted pull her aside and kiss her during lunch period. They certainly didn't need to be caught in the halls by Mr. Armand, the school monitor. I shouldn't let this happen, Chris told herself.

"Wait up, Chris."

Chris quickened her pace and called back, "I just don't want to get in trouble. I mean there are rules about where you go during lunch and where you don't. Those kinds of things are important. What if everybody decided to break the rules? What would happen. . . ."

"Okay, Okay. I just wanted to kiss you, not start a revolution."

Ted had cut in front of Chris and was now walking backwards. He was so quick and graceful, no wonder he'd made quarterback this year on the football team. Chris didn't want it to happen — she tried to look stern — but she could feel a crack appear on her face, the beginning of a smile. Ted laughed, swiftly touching her cheek with the back of his hand, and the smile broke through. Then with a graceful spin on his heels, Ted whipped around, matched Chris's stride, and at the same time draped an arm around her shoulder. They trotted quickly down the stairs until they reached the doorway to the quad, then they paused and looked at each other.

"I'll race you to see whether or not you go to my game today," Ted said.

"Oh, yeah?"

"C'mon."

"No way."

Suddenly Chris burst out of the door and was running for her life. She didn't have to look back to know that Ted was right behind her — he could run circles around just about anybody on the football team. In a moment he had caught up to her and was holding her back by the arm. With a devilish smile he raced ahead, tapped the slim trunk of a newly planted tree, and circled back to her.

"You cheater!!'" Chris cried out. "Ted Mason, you cheater!"

They both laughed until Chris was gasping for air. She bent over at the waist, still giggling, trying to catch her breath.

"I won, I won. You gotta go to the game."

"You didn't win because you didn't play fair, and you know it."

"Who said we had to play fair? I got to the tree first so I won," he replied with a laugh.

Phoebe, still standing next to Brad, watched Chris and Ted panting and laughing in the middle of the quad. When Chris finally stood up and gave a wave, Phoebe couldn't believe how radiant her best friend looked. It was something new, not like the old Chris. The old Chris always had a no-nonsense look in her very blue eyes, a straightforward purposeful gait, and perfect posture. But recently, since she'd started seeing Ted, Chris had a bubbly warmth that softened her and made her all-American beauty absolutely glow. Phoebe saw it again as the couple came near.

"Hi, Pheeb," Chris cried happily, slinging her arm around Phoebe's shoulder. "Do you believe what a cheater this guy is?" Chris shot Ted a look that said, "Don't deny it," and "I'm just teasing," at the same time. But Phoebe barely heard her. Chris touched her gently, "Are you okay? You look kind of sad or something."

Phoebe quickly pasted a smile on her face. "I'm fine. I'm great." Chris looked so happy, Phoebe didn't want to bring her down. She thought back to when she and Chris first met — then it had been Chris who always looked out of sorts.

They had shared an eighth grade locker at Wilson Junior High but were hardly friends. Chris had seemed so cool and austere, and she wouldn't respond to any of Phoebe's attempts to get to know her. It would have stayed that way except for one day when Phoebe raced out during class to fetch a forgotten science book. Chris

17

had also been standing at their locker. At first Phoebe didn't think anything of it. It was only when Phoebe got right next to her that she saw the silent tears pouring down Chris's cheeks.

Without hesitation, Phoebe had taken Chris by the hand and led her to a hidden nook under the stairway. Feeding her Kleenex and peppermint Life Savers, Phoebe listened as Chris emptied her soul. Chris told Phoebe she had just been called "Chris the Priss" by a joking classmate. Chris wanted to do well in school, didn't want to goof off like other kids, and certainly didn't want to disappoint her father.

With a heave Chris told Phoebe something else. Something that had rarely been discussed since. Chris's mother had died of cancer the summer before. Chris missed her. At once, Phoebe began to cry too and put her arms around this girl who had previously been untouchable. A true friendship had begun.

Still, in spite of their closeness, Phoebe didn't know how to explain to Chris this crazy feeling she had. How do you tell your best friend you feel like a bottle of soda pop? Instead, Phoebe looked over at Ted and Brad. They were discussing the upcoming game.

"You ready to play today?" Brad asked.

Ted looked quickly back at Chris. She challenged his glare with one of her own. Ted turned back to Brad and answered, "I can't wait to get a chance at those bozos from Leesberg. I keep hearing how they think they're going to cream us."

18

"Well, last year you guys didn't exactly make them run in terror." Brad laughed.

"Wait, just wait. This year's a whole different number. We've finally got some power in our line. You know, John Marquette, guys like that. And we're really psyched for this game, really psyched. Those Leesberg guys think just because they're cadets at a military academy that they're tougher than we are. Well, they've whipped us once too often. You two coming?"

Brad and Phoebe looked at each other. "I have that senior planning meeting," Brad said. "You going to go Phoebe?"

"I haven't decided yet. Probably." Phoebe didn't really want to go, but she didn't want to disappoint Ted. "Laurie wants to give us a ride," she said, turning to Chris. "Do you want to come?"

Immediately Phoebe sensed that she'd asked the wrong question. Ted cleared his throat and faced his girlfriend. He seemed to challenge her, and Phoebe knew that he and Chris had been arguing about something to do with the game.

"Well, Chris? Are you going to come or not?" Ted wouldn't let Chris look away.

"I told you, it depends."

"Okay. Depends on what?"

"You know what I mean."

It made Phoebe uncomfortable when Chris and Ted began to argue. She didn't understand why they acted this way.

Suddenly Brad stood up. "I'd love to listen to you two fight it out, but I gotta go talk to Mrs.

19

Kellman about writing me a recommendation."

"Another recommendation!" Ted joked, "Brad, you've got to be the most recommended guy in the school. You'd think you were going to go to Princeton or something."

Brad laughed. "Mason, don't let those cadets do any permanent damage. Phoebe, you want to walk me over to Kellman's room?"

Phoebe nodded. "Listen, Chris, I'll wait for you by the flagpole after school. If I'm not there at ten-after you and Laurie go ahead without me. Okay?"

"Okay." Chris smiled.

The two couples waved good-bye, and Chris momentarily forgot her conflict with Ted. Why wasn't everyone like Phoebe, she thought. Phoebe was the warmest, most generous person she had ever known. Even when Chris was irritable or stubborn, Phoebe was always cheerful and even tempered. Yet there was something about Phoebe lately that worried Chris. She couldn't put her finger on it. Chris wondered if she took Phoebe's loving nature for granted. Chris's thoughts were interrupted when Ted tapped her insistently on the shoulder.

"So, why can't you go to my game? That's all I want to know," he demanded.

"I didn't say I couldn't, I said maybe."

"Yeah." Ted laughed. "If you finish your history assignment before two, if Brenda doesn't act up, if your father isn't home for dinner, and if your stepmother says it's okay, and if you're crowned the Miss Teenage America for 19 . . ."

"Ted." Chris tried not to laugh.

"Right, right," he teased, "big toughie just like the boys at Leesberg. Listen, I'm going to get enough of that in the game this afternoon."

Chris looked exasperated. "It's just that Brenda has a big test tomorrow and . . ."

"I thought Brenda might have something to do with this." He paused and sat her down next to him on the bench. Taking her hands in his, Ted began in a quiet, even voice. "Chris, you are not helping. I don't care what your father says. Just because you are going to be the first woman president doesn't mean that Brenda has to be like you."

Chris rested her head in her hands. She felt Ted's warm palm smooth over her back and thought about Brenda. How could she make him understand? Brenda was the stepsister who had come along with her father's remarriage last year. Brenda was as different from Chris and her father as Ted was from the scrappy kids that Brenda hung out with. How could Ted understand the sense of responsibility she felt toward the wayward girl who had been pushed into her life?

"Ted, Brenda has a big history test tomorrow for Mr. Sholeson. You know how hard he is. She's not doing that well in his class. I told you she still hangs out with those weird kids she met when she ran away last year. My father just keeps getting more and more upset about it. I need to help her do better in school."

"I think you'd help her more by bringing her to the game at Leesberg."

Chris rolled her eyes.

"No, I'm serious. Listen to me. It's not just

that I want you to go to the game. I mean I do, but if you accepted Brenda at school and included her with the crowd, I bet it would do a lot more good than trying to make her get an A on Sholeson's dumb test. She'll never get as good grades as you do — nobody will, but if she felt like you weren't embarrassed by her at school it would do a lot for her."

Chris looked into Ted's blue eyes. They matched the collar of the shirt that stuck out from under his faded sweat shirt. "I don't think Brenda would feel comfortable with our crowd. . . ."

"Or is it that you wouldn't feel comfortable in the crowd with Brenda?" Ted's gaze was clear and intent. There was no mischief in his eye now.

Chris let a lock of hair hide her eyes and wondered if he was right. There was a side of her that was embarrassed to be seen with Brenda. After all, her stepsister had run away from home and did hang out with some creepy types. Besides, it wasn't like Brenda was a friend that she had chosen. Brenda had been chosen for her.

"Why don't you give her a chance," Ted said softly. He easily touched her chin with his finger.

Chris flicked back her hair and looked at him again. Then, a slow smile spread across her face. Ted never worried about what other people thought, whether they approved of him or thought he met their standards. He preferred to be his own judge of things.

Suddenly the bell rang. Ted was bending over to shake the blades of grass from his letterman's jacket when he felt Chris's arms wrap around his waist.

22

"Hey, watch it. We're in a public place," he teased. "Well? What about the game. Are you going to come and watch me make those cadets beg for mercy?"

"I just might. But I'm afraid I won't be able to make it alone. I have a special date to set up with a certain stepsister of mine."

Ted smiled. "Not a bad idea. Wish I'd thought of it."

Chris slid one arm around his neck and tickled him in the ribs with the other. "Don't let it go to your head," she whispered.

He tried to tickle her back, but she grabbed him in a hug instead.

Chapter 3

Phoebe was waiting in the front parking lot before school was over. She jumped onto the thick concrete barrier that surrounded the flagpole, then sat cross-legged with her face tilted up to catch the last few rays of sun. She rolled up the sleeves of her cub scout shirt and unbraided her hair. No raw, exploding feeling now, just warm wonderful sun.

In seventh period computer math, Mrs. Parker had sent Phoebe over to the office with a repair request on a broken Apple. Phoebe was often entrusted with missions to the office, deliveries of notes, valuable objects. Today, however, instead of going back for the last few minutes of class, Phoebe took advantage of her trustworthy reputation and walked to freedom and fresh air a few minutes early.

It was a little weird to be out early, and Phoebe cautiously looked around. The large parking lot stretched out in front of her. It was bordered by a long, crowded bicycle rack on one side and the edge of the athletic field on the other. An old yellow bus was slowly pulling out, probably taking the football team to nearby Leesberg. Looking to find the source of a raucous male laugh, Phoebe spotted three boys in an old beat-up Pontiac. When the boys saw her look their way, they slunk even further down in their seats, but Phoebe could still see cigarettes being carelessly flicked out the window.

Phoebe didn't blame them for wanting to goof off that afternoon. Just like the guys in the car, she was glad she was outside and relaxing on such a beautiful day. Right now the whole idea of computers and binary systems made her head ache. Brad had said it was a good idea for her to take the class, even though math had never been one of her strong subjects. Because Phoebe had learned how to use her parents' home computer, Brad assumed that she had some kind of aptitude for it.

That was just like Brad, always trying to convince her that she had practical talents. Phoebe knew the only reason she had learned to use it had been to help him. As far as her aptitude was concerned, Phoebe suspected that knowing how to type up meeting agendas for Brad, and telling the printer how to spit them out, was somehow different than understanding how the whole thing worked. Besides, the only thing Phoebe really liked about computers was when the screen talked back to her and the machine pretended it was a person. But she had never told that to Brad.

There were a lot of things she never told Brad, Phoebe was beginning to realize. Like that she didn't always feel like typing up his notes for him. But he was always so busy, and what better did she have to do? Maybe that was the problem.

Suddenly Phoebe heard someone calling her from behind. The breathy voice was familiar, but for a second Phoebe couldn't place it.

"Phoebe! I haven't seen you for so long. How are you? How is everybody?"

"Lisa! Hi! When did you get back?"

Lisa Chang stood against the bright blue background of the sky and smiled warmly. She was loaded down with books and papers, but it hardly seemed to affect her. Lisa was small and in shape. Even her baggy white sweat suit couldn't hide her obvious strength. Her shiny black hair fell to her shoulders in a perfect straight line.

Dumping her heavy stack on the ground, Lisa ran over to her childhood friend. Phoebe quickly slid down off the barrier and returned Lisa's enthusiasm with a big hug. "You look great! You must have done well in your competition. Did you win?" Phoebe asked excitedly.

With a tug on her white headband, Lisa shrugged modestly. "Well, it wasn't a real competition, it was just an exhibition, so there were no medals or anything. I think I like it that way, then there are no losers either." Lisa tilted her head and smiled.

Phoebe was amazed at her old friend's humility. In a million years she could never imagine Lisa losing. Ever since they were little girls

Phoebe had been in awe of Lisa's discipline and relentless hard work. Now at sixteen, Lisa had a chance of being one of the best figure skaters in the country.

"So are you back for a while?" Phoebe asked. Lisa missed a lot of school to pursue her skating career. Even when she was in school Lisa only went to class half a day and spent most of her time at the ice rink.

Lisa leaned her foot against the barrier wall and stretched. "I don't think I'll be going away again before the Nationals next year. I've got a lot of work to do before then if I expect to place. Plus look at this stack of make-up homework I just got handed."

Phoebe joined Lisa in shooting a disgusted look at the pile of books. She also knew that somehow Lisa always managed to keep her grades high.

"Just give me or Chris a call if you need any help catching up. We'd be glad to help. Besides, we miss you. We never see you anymore."

"I know. I miss you guys, too. It's weird being back in school. Sometimes I forget that anything exists away from the rink. It's good to remember there are other things besides winning medals or making the team, or doing a perfect triple toe loop."

"Yeah, it must be tough," teased Phoebe, "having to wear those awful costumes, and have people applaud for you, and to travel all over the place. I don't see how you can stand it.

Lisa laughed. "I know. I shouldn't complain.

I love it. Here I am my first day in school again, and I can't wait for my mom to drive me back over to the rink."

Cars were starting to pull in along the front of the school, and Lisa paused to see if her mother's was among them. "How's Brad?"

"Great. Really busy. You know."

"Why don't you two come by the rink some afternoon and say hello. I get to stop for a hot chocolate every once in a while. I'm there every single afternoon except Wednesdays when I have ballet class."

"Maybe we will." Phoebe spotted Mrs. Chang waving as she pulled into the other end of the parking lot. Phoebe waved back. "Your mom's here. Tell her I said hi."

"Sure. Give Brad a big hug hello for me. Remember, come and visit me at the rink. Bye!" Lisa yelled as the bell rang. She seemed to be saying something else about Brad, but Phoebe couldn't hear it above the roar that was filling the parking lot as kids poured out the front doors of the school.

Phoebe climbed back up on the barrier to wait for Chris. She watched Lisa's strong, focused body race across the parking lot. Phoebe envied that sense of purpose and couldn't remember the last time she'd been in such a hurry to get anywhere. Something about seeing Lisa had made that feeling come back with a painful intensity. Phoebe was beginning to realize that she couldn't go on feeling this way forever. Something had to change. That was all there was to it. She wasn't sure what it was, but something had to change.

"Brenda," Chris whispered determinedly, "where are you, Brenda?"

As soon as she heard the bell, Chris rushed out to find her stepsister. Although she didn't like to admit it, she usually tried to avoid running into Brenda at school. But Ted was right, tutoring Brenda for tests and pretending that she was helping her stepsister fit into her new environment was not enough. Chris had to get over her discomfort at her stepsister's rebellious personality and give her a chance.

Chris knew that Brenda's last class was PE and raced over to the gym hoping to catch her. Laurie was going to leave at ten after so there wasn't much time. She parked herself outside the locker room entrance and hoped she wasn't too late.

Girls were just starting to file out. Noticing their wet hair, Chris remembered that Brenda had swimming this semester. Each time the locker room doors opened the chlorine smell wafted out and the hum of hair dryers competed with shrill laughter.

A group of six or seven girls came through the doors, each pausing to say hello to Chris. Brenda was the last girl in the group. She didn't stop and didn't say hello.

"Brenda, wait up," Chris offered tentatively. Brenda stopped but did not turn around.

Chris quickly jogged around to face her stepsister. Assuming a defensive posture, Brenda put a hand on her hip and leaned into it. Her dark brown hair was very wet and slicked back. Even

29

though she hadn't redone her makeup, her features were sharp and clearly defined: high cheekbones, wide mouth, sharp slender nose. The redness from the chlorine and the remnants of black mascara smudged underneath made her eyes look even larger than usual.

"Um, hi," Chris offered.

Brenda made the slightest response with a flick of her head.

"What are you doing this afternoon?" Chris continued.

"Why?" answered Brenda in a flat, suspicious voice. Brenda was very wary of Chris. There had been many fights at home about where Brenda went after school and who she hung out with, and Chris was always on the same side as her father.

Brenda was still very close to kids at a halfway house in Georgetown, the house that she had run away to after her mother had married Chris's father. Since all of those kids had family problems, neither Chris nor her father nor Brenda's mother approved of the association, and Brenda took it hard. With a tug on her oversized dark sweater, Brenda began to walk along the edge of the athletic field.

Chris heaved a sigh and followed. She wondered if Ted was wrong. Maybe the best thing to do was just to leave Brenda alone. That seemed to be what her stepsister wanted.

"Brenda," said Chris with forced patience, "I am going to go to Ted's football game this afternoon. It's over at Leesberg Military." Chris was still a step behind her stepsister and couldn't see her face. "Would you like to come with me?"

Brenda stopped walking. She turned and squinted at Chris as if she hadn't heard her correctly. "You want me to go to a football game with you?"

"Sure." Chris tried to sound casual. "I have a ride to take us over there. It'll be fun. Come on."

Brenda looked down at her boots and made circles in the dirt. "Is your whole crowd going?"

"I don't know. Phoebe might go. I'm sure lots of other kids I know will be there, if that's what you mean."

Brenda looked over towards the parking lot and back down to her boots. "I have that test for Sholeson tomorrow."

"Well, if you have to study, that comes first. I understand. Um, maybe next game we'll go together. Okay?" Chris tried to hide her sense of relief.

Brenda nodded. "I mean, I look kind of grubby from swimming."

"We'll do it another time," Chris repeated.

"But if you really want me to go . . ." Brenda stopped mid-sentence and looked her stepsister in the eye for the first time. "I mean, I guess I could finish studying tonight. I don't have all that much left to do."

"If you're sure you'll have enough time."

"Okay. I mean, sure, I'll go."

Chris stood there for a minute before it sank in. Brenda actually wanted to go to the game with her. Never before had Chris offered to share her social life, and now she felt embarrassed at the obvious slight her stepsister must have been feeling.

"I could help you study later" — Chris paused — "that is, if you want me to."

"Yeah, sure, that would be good." Brenda ran her hands through her wet hair until it fell in long layered wisps around her face. She wet both her pinkies and rubbed under her eyes. "Do I still have smudges?"

"No, you look fine."

Brenda managed a reserved smile.

Phoebe knew she wasn't going to the game. It was the last place she wanted to spend the afternoon. She wasn't sure where she was headed, but she hopped down off the wall and walked back in towards the center of campus.

It was starting to make sense to her, this panic, this feeling. It was because she was lost! Look at Lisa. No wonder seeing Lisa after so long had made that feeling burst out. Lisa was a perfect example of everything Phoebe wasn't. She had achieved something unusual and difficult. When you thought of Lisa you automatically thought of skating. That was Lisa's identity, that was what made Lisa special.

It was the same with all her friends. They could be described in few words, and the listener would know they were someone to pay attention to. But who was she? How could anyone describe her? Brad's girl friend was the only label Phoebe could come up with, and she knew that wasn't enough. Brad probably thought it was okay, but

Phoebe knew that other friends like Woody would agree with her.

Woody had always told her that you had to make yourself special, make the effort to do something important or different. He had always told her she was special, but that she had to take that specialness and make something out of it. He always said no one else could do it for her.

Phoebe was starting to feel calmer, the tightness in her throat was gone. Replacing the tension was a humming, which felt warm and happy as it filled her head. Soon Phoebe was singing to herself and walking briskly across the quad.

She knew where she was going now. When she looked at the white wooden steps, a smile took over her face and her eyes opened wide. She was standing in front of the Little Theater and the auditions for the Follies had just begun.

Chapter
4

Outside in the parking lot, Chris and Brenda stopped to look for their ride. "Who are we driving over with?" asked Brenda huskily. Cars were lined up waiting to pull out into the street, and the air was clouded with exhaust fumes.

"Laurie Bennington. I don't know if you know her."

Brenda chewed on her thumbnail and shrugged. It was a big school and almost impossible to know everyone in your class. She reached in her shoulder bag and slid on a pair of sunglasses that gave a toughness to her delicate face.

A bright red van pulled up next to them, and a girl with long, wavy hair and pale, translucent skin stuck her head out the window. It was Sasha Jenkins.

"Hi, Chris," Sasha shouted happily. "Brenda, hi. Are you taking art again this semester?"

"No," answered Brenda with a shake of her wet hair.

"Me neither. I'm too busy with the newspaper for much else extra. Do you guys need a ride to the game?"

"No thanks," Chris yelled back. "See you over there. Give Ted a good write-up."

Sasha gave a thumbs-up as the van pulled away. Chris wondered if she shouldn't have taken Sasha up on her offer of a ride. Brenda had never really been around anyone in the crowd before, and Chris was nervous about how her friends would react. Sasha had been friendly. Of course, Sasha was always sweet and open. Even in her articles in the paper, she was always the first to defend the underdog. But, Chris had promised Laurie that she would ride with her, and Laurie had been making such an effort to be friends that Chris didn't want to insult her.

"Chris!!!" A voice cool as cut glass could suddenly be heard over the roar. Laurie Bennington was standing inside the open door of her white Mustang convertible and leaning against the frame. She gave a hearty wave and then quickly sat down behind the steering wheel.

"That's Laurie," Chris announced. The two girls walked toward the car.

When they got closer to the shiny Mustang, they could see a boy sitting in the front passenger seat. Laurie was turned attentively toward him, her perfect legs tucked under her and her hem riding up her thigh. Leaning towards him, Laurie's one long earring dangled against her chin. The boy was carefully examining a plastic box of cassette tapes. Chris was surprised to see it was Peter Lacey, DJ for the school radio station.

"Hey, Chris," Peter said in his slight New Jersey accent. "I dedicated a song to Ted and the team today. It was called "Make 'em Run for Cover," by the Ruby Blues. Stinko song, but I thought it might help the killer instinct."

Chris had to laugh. Peter was one of the cuter boys in the crowd. He was wearing a sleeveless sweatshirt with "Victory Tour" written across it. It was hard to ignore the sharp muscle definition in his arm.

Chris wondered if Laurie was making a play for Peter. He was usually too involved in his beloved radio station to notice the many girls who tried to get his attention. Of course, Laurie was different from other girls.

Laurie wriggled into her seat and adjusted her dress. Chris noticed Laurie carefully watching Peter out of the corner of her eye. If she was trying to get his attention, it didn't seem to be working. He was totally immersed in the box full of cassette tapes, not the gorgeous girl next to him.

"Laurie," began Chris, "do you know my stepsister, Brenda? She's going to come to the game with us." Chris looked around to introduce Brenda but her stepsister had somehow disappeared in the last few seconds. Then, with a flash of anger, Chris spotted her. Brenda had backed up and was sitting on the front fender of the car behind them. Her posture was a mixture of pretended cool and outright hostility. Between her dark glasses and defensive attitude she looked like a poster girl for a motorcycle gang. Chris felt a wave of embarrassment as she watched Laurie look at Brenda with disapproval.

"Oh, Brenda. Hi," Laurie said finally after the pause. "I've heard all about you." Laurie turned away and reached over Peter. She pulled a pair of driving gloves from the glove compartment. Slowly tugging the gloves onto her hands, she turned back and looked Brenda up and down. Then she cleared her throat. "Listen, Chris, I'd love to give Brenda a ride, but Phoebe's coming, too, and there really isn't room for five with all our books and everything. I mean, there's room for you, but you should have let me know earlier about Brenda. You understand, don't you?" Laurie's voice was dripping with sweetness.

"Laurie." Chris tried to sound offhand. She didn't know Laurie very well and wasn't quite sure how to react. "I don't think Phoebe's coming with us. She's obviously not here, and she said only to wait until ten after, so I'm sure she went on home. So, there's no problem right?"

Laurie glared. "Well, even so, you know that there are seats being saved for us at Leesberg, and I don't think there will be room for Brenda to sit with us if she did come along."

Peter was still bent over the box but had stopped looking at the tapes.

"Brenda and I will find our own seats. You don't have to worry about it. Really, Laurie."

Chris knew that Laurie had a snobby side, but hadn't realized she could be so obvious, so cruel. After all, Brenda was standing right there next to them.

"Come on, Laur, what's the big deal? We can squeeze together," interrupted Peter. Immediately he went back to his tapes and put one in the cassette deck. The new-wave song only made the atmosphere more tense.

Laurie looked back at Peter and gave a suggestive laugh. "I guess we could. Sorry. I just didn't want to leave Phoebe behind after I told her I'd give her a ride."

Chris knew that Laurie was backtracking now. She wondered if Laurie was only changing her tune to please Peter. It certainly seemed that way.

Chris opened the door and climbed in the back. In a second she realized that Brenda was not following. Frozen, Brenda stood next to the other car holding her books in front of her like a shield. She came over to the driver's side to face Laurie, but her words were obviously meant for Chris. "I've changed my mind," she said tersely, her eyes hidden by her dark glasses. "I really didn't want to go to any stupid football game anyway." As an afterthought she leaned in and added, "You know what, Laurie Bennington? You know where you can go." With that, Brenda spun around on the heel of her boot and stalked off towards the street. Chris, Peter, and Laurie sat there without speaking until at last Laurie angrily turned off the tape deck.

"Cute. Very cute," Laurie spat out.

Chris sighed. "Laurie, you could have been friendlier. You didn't have to make it so obvious that you didn't want her to go."

"I said she could come with us."

"I know, but . . ."

"Well, didn't I?" Laurie's voice had risen so that its sound was like a frying pan being dropped on the floor. Even Peter was startled, his usually absorbed, cool look replaced by an expression of concern and slight disgust. The tone of her voice kept right on.

"Look, Chris," she zeroed in, "all I've heard is what a jerk she is. I've heard she was into drugs and gross stuff like that. How do you expect me to react when you suddenly show up with her. Come on! She walks over here looking like some totally sleazoid weirdo, acting like she's angry at the whole world. I mean maybe I wasn't very nice, but what am I supposed to do? Pretend like I want to make her my best friend? Then I offer her a ride and she tells me off. Really!"

"I know," Chris squeaked.

"Let's go. We're going to miss the beginning of the game." Laurie started the engine.

"Wait. I'm not going to go, Laur. Thanks, but I'd better go home and talk this out with Brenda," Chris explained. She was hardly in the mood now to cheer at a football game.

As Peter raised his seat so Chris could slide out his door, Laurie put her hand out to stop her. "You're not mad at me, are you, Chris?" Her voice was much, much softer now. "I'm sorry. I didn't mean to hurt her feelings. You kind of caught me off guard. I mean, it's no reflection on you. You know how much I like you."

"It's okay, Laurie. I understand."

"Are you sure? Do you promise you're not mad at me?"

"I promise." Chris nodded. "Bye, Peter. Cheer Ted on for me."

"Okay," Peter said. His eyes were not for a moment deflected from Laurie. Chris couldn't figure out whether he agreed with Laurie or was appalled by her. That was okay; Chris couldn't figure Laurie out either.

After she left school, Brenda wasn't quite sure where she was walking, but she knew one thing — she really despised Laurie Bennington. And she blamed Chris. Chris had set her up for that humiliation. She'd looked on while Laurie made her snide comments and well . . . Brenda wasn't sure what to think about her stepsister, but she was really angry.

Brenda thought back over the last year. She had been pleased when her mother had announced she was going to marry the widower whom she'd met only weeks before. But everything had gone wrong. Chris was controlled, beautiful, accomplished. She wasn't unfriendly or anything, just kind of intimidating. And Brenda felt so awkward around her, especially, since she felt that Chris looked at her as a loser.

The lowest time had been right after the marriage when Brenda and her mother moved to

Rose Hill. Brenda loathed the atmosphere of the wealthy suburb — it was all surface and money and phoniness. Brenda thought she'd never seen so many spoiled kids in her life, and there was her stepsister hobnobbing with the best of them. Even though Kennedy was famous for producing more Regents scholars, Ivy Leaguers, and National Merit finalists than any other public school in the eastern United States, Brenda thought it was overrated.

The worst was that Chris's father felt Brenda had been too loosely brought up and took it upon himself to make his stepdaughter take a more serious approach to school and her own future. And her mom actually took his side. Using achiever Chris as an example of what Brenda should be striving for, Mr. Austin — with Brenda's mom in full support — began setting down rules and expectations regarding her schoolwork and grades. He checked to make sure that each assignment was up to his standards and made it very clear that Brenda was supposed to break ties with her old companions, kids who hung out on the streets and in the parks of D.C. Meanwhile, Chris was held up to Brenda as a paragon of virtue.

Brenda just couldn't take it. After an argument with her mother and stepfather she had headed for the streets of Washington and had ended up staying at a halfway house where she made a lot of friends. Chris, her parents, and of course everybody else at Kennedy were appalled.

Big deal, Brenda thought to herself walking swiftly down the street. They didn't know her friends at the halfway house; they really had no idea what they were talking about. They had this image in their heads of what her friends were like — how they drank and smoked, took drugs, and were "loose." That image was way off, but Brenda got tired of trying to convince them. Tired of all the Laurie Bennington weirdos in the world, the snobs, the gossips, and the phonies.

Still, Brenda suspected that Chris wasn't that way. Sometimes she really did seem to try. But trying didn't count for Brenda anymore, she'd been insulted too many times by people with condescending smiles. And now, even a small incident like today's made her feel terrible. When she thought about it, she was really much too angry to face Chris.

Brenda rounded another corner walking fiercely toward downtown Rose Hill and still not knowing where she wanted to go.

Meanwhile, farther behind, Chris quickly traveled the mile and a half home. The impressive colonial and brick houses that lined the streets made her feel more purposeful, more resolved to set things straight with her new sister. It was true that Laurie Bennington was uppity, but Brenda had to learn not to fly off the handle and act like a two-year-old every time someone snubbed her.

Why had Brenda come along and messed up her neatly arranged life? They had to talk about it, they had to get things straight. Laurie had been nasty, but Brenda shouldn't have overreacted. There were certain ways of doing things, and Brenda hadn't caught on. It was all so frustrating. And Chris was angry, maybe even too angry to talk to Brenda. Well, she'd have to try anyway.

Chris took a deep, determined breath and headed swiftly for home.

Chapter
5

Phoebe sat down on the front steps outside the Little Theater and listened to the tag end of Woody's pep talk through the open door. His excited voice sailed easily over the last row of eager auditioners, and she could understand every word. She'd wanted to catch Woody alone, just to say hi and give him a big, friendly smile, but listening to him from out here was almost as good. His warm, familiar voice made her forget about her strange, unsettled feelings.

"Okay, guys!" she heard him call. "The sign-up list is posted on the back wall, and we'll go in order. Karen will let you know when you're next. Karen, stand up so everybody knows who you are."

Phoebe smiled as a light round of applause greeted what must have been Karen identifying herself. Karen Carlson was a heavy-set junior who knew a lot about sets and lights and usually acted as Woody's stage manager.

"Randy Nakamora is the pianist if you need accompaniment. He's great, so if you make a mistake, don't blame it on the piano player." There was some nervous laughter and another round of applause. "Get ready to go on stage while the group before you is auditioning. If you want to rehearse, go outside and keep the yakking down when other people are on. When you get up on the stage, say your name or the name of your group and what you're going to be performing. Get it? Okay!!! Have a good time, break a leg, and gooood luck!!!"

Phoebe jumped out of the way as kids began to pour nervously out into the quad. The first girl out was Joanie Lavelle, a tall black girl in a maroon leotard with a pink sweatshirt tied around her waist. She immediately went over to the nearest bench and began using the back of it as a ballet barre. Joanie was followed by Chris Jenkins and Pat Patton who were going over the words of the classic comedy routine, "Who's on First?"

Phoebe quietly stepped behind the stairs and leaned on the wooden railing. As the rest of the kids poured out of the theater the quad began to look like a circus. The "Breakers and Poppers" started rehearsing a nervy looking break-dance routine on one side and Blue Moon, six seniors who sang and danced to fifties songs, were in formation on the other. Phoebe heard a loud, slightly off-key soprano and recognized Jane

McGraw singing along with her walkman. Next to Jane were seniors Jim Garcia and the Price twins, whose juggling act had been a standard part of the Follies since they'd been at Kennedy. They were giving tips to Darrell Boldt who hoped to combine juggling with his comedy routine about life at Kennedy High.

Phoebe couldn't remember when she'd seen this much life in the Kennedy quad. A big, goofy smile warmed her face as she watched a pair of scared freshmen going over dance steps and counting the beats to "Putting on the Ritz." At the same time a guitar was being strummed, a banjo plucked, and something that sounded like a saxophone was being ineptly blasted from behind the bushes.

Good old Woody, thought Phoebe. Nobody else could inspire this kind of energy and enthusiasm. She could imagine him inside the theater, pacing up and down the aisles, clipboard in hand, pencil in mouth, his forehead lined with concentration as he got ready to give each performer an equal chance. She had even seen him unconsciously mouth the words to a song someone else was singing as if he could will the performer to sing it just a little bit better.

"Joan Lavelle," announced the stage manager, Karen, from the doorway. Joan shook out her hands and picked up a small tape recorder she had set on the bench. Her face was stern with concentration as she ran up the steps and into the Little Theater.

"Darrell, you're next," added Karen and pulled the door shut. Darrell immediately dropped his juggling balls. A blue one bounced off the stairs and all the way over to the other end of the quad.

Music started, a fuzzy recording of the theme from *Flashdance*. Phoebe wished she could go in and watch Joanie dance, but she knew it would be breaking Woody's professional rules to open the door in the middle of someone's performance. Closing her eyes, she tried to imagine the acrobatic movements Joanie was probably performing and found herself singing along with the music. It was not really the kind of song she'd choose to perform, but the rhythm filled her with pleasure.

"Excuse me."

Phoebe felt a warm hand rest lightly on her forearm. Startled, she turned sharply and looked into a pair of gray-blue eyes that she had never seen before.

"You're a beautiful singer. Can I ask your advice? I'm having trouble with this one part of my song. Could you listen to me for a second?" he asked.

Phoebe didn't answer for a moment. The boy looked a little older than she and was lanky and long limbed. His light brown hair framed a boyish, sensitive face that seemed both wise and full of fun. What made Phoebe pause was the boy's eyes. They had just a slight twinkle.

"Well?" the boy asked after a moment of silence.

"Oh, oh, I'm sorry. Um, sure I could listen to you."

"Great! Could you come over here where it's quieter?"

He led her in the opposite direction from the quad, toward the art building. "Thanks. I really appreciate it. It was easy singing along with the record at home, but now, looking at this sheet music, I'm not sure I have the melody right. It's kind of confusing."

Phoebe was still wondering what she was getting herself into, but she was also fascinated and flattered. This boy apparently thought she was some kind of expert. They sat down under a tree and spread the sheet music out on the grass between them. The song was "Sweet Beginnings," a pop ballad Phoebe had on a favorite album at home.

"You mean you've never gone over it with an accompanist?" Phoebe asked. "You know, the sheet music could be really different from the way the song sounds on the record. You should have gotten a musician to play it for you before the audition." Phoebe scanned the pages of musical notes. She had picked up the ability to read music more quickly than anyone else in choir.

The boy moved closer. "I figured I'd just wing it. What's important is the feeling and the mood. If you get the heart of the song, nobody's going to care if a few notes are off. Right?" He started to sing the verse in a light, melodic voice.

"I guess. I never quite thought of it that way." Phoebe looked at the boy again, but he was involved in the music. He wore a faded blue button-down shirt and a pair of old Levis, with his watch hanging from one of the belt loops of his pants. There was a flush of pink just under his cheekbones. Phoebe had never noticed him at school before. She wondered why.

"Here it is." He pointed to a bar in the music. "I can't remember how this one part goes." He sang, "Since the beginning of time . . ."

His singing was musical and full of feeling. But he was right, something about the melody was a touch off.

Phoebe looked at the music for a moment. "One more time."

Without hesitation, the boy began again, "Since the beginning of time, it's the same old hope . . ."

"Nope. It's not quite right."

"Darn. I knew it!"

Phoebe leaned forward. "Listen." She sang softly, "Since the beginning of time, it's the same old hope . . ." She slowed down on the last few words, making sure that he heard the notes. "Hear that? 'Same old hope' . . ." she sang again. "Got it?"

"I think so. Sing it with me."

"Since the beginning of time, it's the same old hope . . ." they sang together.

"That's good. You're getting closer. Try it again."

More lines, more melody. The boy didn't give up. Finally, it came out perfectly.

"That's it." Phoebe clapped her hands happily.

"Great, great. Sing with me from there until the end."

49

Phoebe nodded and started singing. They read the music together and when they came to the end of the song, they both naturally went back to the beginning again. This time, Phoebe couldn't resist adding some harmony and the boy followed her inflections. Then, in the middle of the song, they switched parts instinctively, without telling each other. He suddenly switched to the harmony and she to the melody. When the song was over they both started to laugh.

"That was amazing! You are a really incredible singer!" The boy shook his head in appreciation.

A voice broke through from around the quad. "Griffin Neill. Griffin . . ."

Karen walked up to the boy and checked her list. "You're next. After Blue Moon. They take about ten minutes, so you can wait another five or so if you want."

"Thanks." Griffin smiled nervously. Karen headed back to the theater.

"I guess your name is Griffin Neill."

"Well, I guess so." They both laughed and Griffin extended his hand. "What's your name?"

"Phoebe Hall."

Griffin looked at her hard with his searching blue-gray eyes. "Listen, Phoebe Hall. When are you auditioning?"

"I wasn't really going to audition. I just. . . ."

"What? You have to audition. You have such a good voice. Hey, let's do "Sweet Beginnings" as a duet! I think we sound pretty good together and that you definitely increase my chances of success."

Why was he asking her to do this? She had already decided the Follies would be a waste of time. She could still hear Brad telling her how the show was dumb and a joke, but somehow, his words were beginning to fade. She really wanted to try out now that she was here, she wanted to try out very badly. She looked up at Griffin's expectant face and felt a shot of warmth rush through her.

In that moment, Phoebe knew she'd do it. It was as though that shot of warmth had flattened the fizz and left her free to decide what it was she really wanted to do.

"How about this," Phoebe spouted. "We could divide up lines of the first half of the song between us, each one singing a phrase or two alone. Then we could do our harmony in the second part."

"Great! Let's figure it out. We'd better hurry. We have exactly five minutes."

Phoebe and Griffin raced through the music so quickly that when they walked up the steps to the theater, Phoebe had no idea which lines she was supposed to sing, which to harmonize, or what. Waiting for Blue Moon to finish, her stomach did its famous pancake flip, but at least there was no exploding feeling. She was nervous, however, about her own bright idea of dividing up the lines, since it meant that she would have to sing alone at certain points.

There was a smattering of applause at the end of Blue Moon's rendition of "Johnny Angel." When Karen opened the door, Phoebe couldn't believe how full the small auditorium was. Most of the kids had given up on last-minute rehearsing efforts and come in to watch. The sight of all those people made Phoebe's heart pump even faster.

"Let's go," whispered Griffin. He almost ran to the stage ahead of her, he was that anxious to get up there. Phoebe walked slowly, suddenly wishing for an honorable way to back out.

Woody was bent over his clipboard, madly scribbling, and didn't look up until he heard Phoebe's voice quietly announce her name.

"Phoeberooni!" he gushed with surprise and involuntary warmth. As soon as the word was out of his mouth, he looked around to see if anyone had noticed his obvious favoritism. When Phoebe smiled back at him, her coppery hair reflecting the makeshift lights, Woody gave her a wink that was filled with affection.

Griffin handed the music to Randy at the piano and rejoined Phoebe center stage. When Randy started playing, Phoebe really had no idea if it was her turn to sing or not. She gave Griffin a panicked look, and then he sang the first line. His voice was even stronger and clearer than it had been outside. But Phoebe felt stuck. They had planned it too quickly. Now she wasn't even sure of the words.

Then, Phoebe felt Griffin take her hand in his with a steady but gentle grip. She turned to face him, and his eyes locked on hers. He seemed to be saying, don't think about the audience, just sing to me. His eyes were beautiful and calm.

There was no fear in them, just complete confidence.

Concentrating on Griffin's blue-gray eyes, Phoebe relaxed and took a deep breath. When he finished his line, she sang. The voice almost didn't feel like her own, yet she heard the music soaring. Griffin answered each line as if they were having a passionate conversation. By the time they began the harmony, there was no audience for Phoebe, no Woody, nothing but her voice and Griffin's voice blending in some beautiful place that she seldom got to visit. When the song ended, Phoebe was surprised. Griffin let go of her hand and everyone in the auditorium began to applaud.

The applause was loud and long and Phoebe felt light, almost giddy. Woody was beaming at her. When she got off the stage and sat down with the rest of the audience, she began to shake with excitement. She couldn't help grinning. She wanted to thank Griffin for his help, but he was already walking back down the aisle on his way out. He turned for a split second to wave good-bye and slipped out the door. He was gone.

Phoebe sat through the rest of the auditions enjoying each act immensely, whether it was really good or not. She just felt so full and free that no one could do anything wrong.

The afternoon ended with Woody thanking everyone and announcing that he would post a list of those selected for the show on Monday. He tried to ignore Phoebe and pretend she was just like everyone else, but before he left, he couldn't resist coming up to her and whispering.

"You were the best, Pheeb, the absolute best."

Phoebe laughed it off, as if it were a joke, but inside she knew she had just done something that was special. And that realization made her feel absolutely terrific.

Chapter
6

Phoebe jogged along the streets, her book bag bouncing against her back with a rhythmic thump. She didn't usually like to run, but she felt so light, so energized, so incredibly full of life that to travel at a mere walk was impossible.

Chris lived on one of the newer streets in Rose Hill. The house was an elegant, modern two-story painted a dull grayish blue. The front yard sloped so steeply that it was useless for anything but growing ivy. Phoebe panted up the concerte stairs and banged the huge brass knocker.

When Chris opened the door, Phoebe knew immediately that something was wrong. Chris had that expression on her face — her mouth was formed in a hard little line and her eyes looked around Phoebe as if she didn't quite expect her friend to be the only one there.

"Hi, Phoebe," she said abruptly.

"Hi. Is it okay that I came by?"

Chris smiled briefly and opened the door even wider. "Of course. It's just one of those days."

"Really?"

"Yeah, if you can stand it, come on in and I'll tell you more than you'll ever want to know."

Phoebe laughed. No matter how rotten a mood Chris was in, it wasn't going to bother her. She felt good enough for both of them. "How was the game?" she ventured.

Chris frowned. "I didn't go."

Phoebe nodded. That had to be bad mood reason number one. The rest of the reasons would follow, and Phoebe had a feeling that they just might include Brenda.

Chris guided Phoebe down the long, brick entryway of the Austin family home. It was done in the best Washington Federalist style. The hallway led out to a huge living room that actually had big bay windows looking out over the whole west side of town. Every time Phoebe saw the view, it impressed her.

"Why don't you stay for dinner?" Chris offered. "I'll ask Catherine if it's okay." Chris couldn't quite bring herself to call her stepmother "Mom."

While Chris pushed through a swinging door into the kitchen, Phoebe sank down on the plush white sofa. She found that she was still humming "Sweet Beginnings." Again, Phoebe felt an irrepressible smile erupt. It was as if she were sitting on some wonderful secret that was bubbling inside her. Chris stuck her head out of the kitchen and nodded to Phoebe that dinner was on. Phoebe picked up the princess telephone on the end table and called home.

"Hi, Ma, I'm going to eat dinner at Chris's." Phoebe was amazed how lively her house sounded even over the phone. Shawn's stereo was blasting, and she could hear her mom was printing out something on the computer. That reminded her, she had to print up Brad's meeting agenda tonight.

"Great, hon," said Mrs. Hall hurriedly. "Daddy's staying late at the office, and I'm trying to finish typing a brief for him here, so tonight it's peanut butter sandwiches for Shawn and me." Phoebe's father was a lawyer, and her mom was his secretary. "If you can get Mrs. Austin to feed you a decent meal, be my guest. But, sweetheart, be home by eight-thirty if you want to use the computer. Daddy will need it later tonight." Her mom smacked a kiss over the phone and hung up.

As Phoebe put down the receiver, Chris came out of the kitchen with her stepmother. Instinctively, Phoebe sat up straighter and moved her dirty book bag off the shiny maple coffee table and onto the floor.

Chris was taller than her father's gentle new wife. Blonder and sturdier, too. Mrs. Austin had a delicate fading beauty marred by prematurely gray hair and deep lines under her tired eyes. Phoebe always wondered if bringing up Brenda by herself had caused Mrs. Austin to age so harshly. Something about Chris's stepmother was so sweet and refined that it was hard to imagine her standing up to a rebellious daughter like Brenda.

"Phoebe, dear, it's lovely that you're joining us for supper," she said with a faint Boston accent. She gave Chris a look that seemed to imply that somehing was wrong. "Chris, why don't you take your friend upstairs and do some homework. I'll call you when your father gets home."

With that, Phoebe scooped up her things, and she and Chris bounded up the long waxed staircase and into Chris's bedroom.

"Gee, are you sure it was okay for me to stay for dinner? Catherine looked a little mad or something," Phoebe speculated as she tossed her books on the floor and stretched out on one of the matching twin beds. The warmth inside her was still strong, and she felt like lounging and purring like a cat.

"It's Brenda . . . again."

"Bad?"

Chris rolled her eyes and then sat down cross-legged on the floor. She retold the whole story starting with the parking lot, going on with Laurie, and ending where Chris wasn't quite sure. "Something has got to give," was her final analysis. "She just can't go on acting like the whole school has some kind of conspiracy against her."

Phoebe agreed. "It sounds like she did overreact. Have you seen her yet?"

"No. I came right home to talk it out, but she wasn't here. She's still not home, and Catherine thinks she might have gone to Georgetown to see her creepo friends — which my dad has told her not to do. It's a big, huge mess."

"Sounds like it, although I do have some sympathy for Brenda. I'm starting to get the feeling that Laurie can be a real pain sometimes."

"That's not the point," asserted Chris. "Brenda has to stop acting like a baby. It's not fair to any of us. Anything goes wrong, and she blows up. It's ridiculous. I don't know where she learned to get away with it. Maybe from her weirdo friends in D.C., I don't know. They're all out of it, if you ask me."

"And you aren't?" Phoebe teased. Suddenly, the grin that she had been trying to hold back burst out in a hearty laugh. Chris sat rigidly straight in her desk chair and looked at her red-headed friend as if she had lost her mind.

"What's with you, Hall? Hey, how come you didn't go to the game? Why are you acting so goony?" Chris tossed a pillow at her.

Phoebe just continued to smirk and grabbed the pillow in a robust hug. She knew she was acting like a total fool, but she couldn't help it. It had been a long time since she'd felt this light and giddy. It was just the opposite of holding in that awful fizziness. This was the pure laughing gas of knowing that she'd just done something special and done it very well.

"I auditioned for the Follies, for Woody! I think I'm going to get to sing a song in the show!" Phoebe explained enthusiastically. She started to tell Chris about Griffin but stopped herself. She was afraid it might come out wrong and sound like . . . she wasn't sure what it was she was afraid of sounding like. She tried to reassure herself. It wasn't meeting Griffin that was making her so excited, it was the thrill of being in the show.

"What fantastic news, Phoebe. That's great. I love hearing you sing," Chris said, a little brighter now. "Do you think Brad will mind?"

"He'd only mind if it meant I couldn't go to Princeton with him. Since that's got nothing to do with it, he won't mind," Phoebe added, trying to convince herself she was right. The question made her feel a little more somber. "At least I hope he won't," Phoebe added, this time with a tinge of apprehension.

"Well, if Brad *is* mad, we can both be in hot water together. I'm sure Ted's really furious at me because I didn't go to his game at Leesberg. Maybe if our team wins, he won't mind as much." Both girls stared off in different directions.

"I hope Brad and I don't have a fight," said Phoebe, hugging the pillow even tighter. "I hate fighting."

"Yeah, I know what you mean," echoed Chris.

Dinner at the Austin house was formal and serious. Phoebe was never quite sure which fork to use or if she was supposed to help clear the table or just sit there. Chris's father, a political analyst, started off the meal with a lecture on the importance of getting into the right college. He was trying to steer the conversation toward

politics when Brenda slipped through the swinging doors and sat down. The moment was very
dramatic because everybody was doing their best
to pretend it wasn't happening.

Brenda set a place for herself and began
piling food onto her plate. She said please and
thank you, even complimented her mother on
the cooking, and seemed to ignore the fact that
showing up so late for dinner was unusual at all.
A lock of wavy dark hair hid her eyes, and
Phoebe thought that if a person could actually
eat defiantly, Brenda was managing to do it.

"Where did you go after school, Brenda?"
Mrs. Austin finally asked calmly.

"That's my business," Brenda replied. After
the briefest glance at Chris, she immediately
shifted her eyes back to her plate.

Catherine gave her husband a pleading look.
Phoebe realized the adults didn't want any scenes,
especially in front of a guest. That would be a
definite no-no around the Austin place. Everything was played by strict rules.

"Brenda, we'll talk after supper. I looked over
your essay for English class and I'd like to discuss
that with you, too," said Mr. Austin. Brenda
didn't respond. He resumed his chat about cur-
rent events, but in a way, Phoebe thought
Brenda's silent treatment was working better
than ever. Who could concentrate on dinner or
politics when there was a silent revolution taking
place across the candelabra?

Finally, over dessert, Brenda lifted her eyes
for what seemed like the first time. She looked

like a deer in the woods, lovely, suspicious and always on guard.

"How was the football game?" Brenda asked her sister in a smoky voice.

Chris tensed. "I didn't go to the football game. I came straight home because I wanted to talk to you about what happened. But then you weren't here." The last remark was on an accusatory note, and Phoebe could almost feel the electricity in her fork. Chris was tight and controlled, but playing a dangerous game. Her parents exchanged looks.

Brenda's eyes flickered. "What's there to talk about?"

Chris put down her teacup. "For starters, what about you talking to me or Dad or Catherine when something upsets you instead of running off to see your friends."

"Girls, let's discuss this later. We have a dinner guest," said Mr. Austin in an overly tight voice. Chris immediately nodded and sat back silently in her chair.

But Brenda wanted to keep going. She threw down her napkin. "You think my friends are such lowlifes just because they may have had a few problems. Well, as far as I can see, they're a lot better than someone like Laurie Bennington. She has everything anyone could want or need, and she can't even be a decent human being. Chris, you don't have to worry. I'll try not to embarrass you again in front of people like Laurie, who you look up to so much."

Then, all Phoebe heard was Brenda's chair

scraping against the polished wooden floor and footsteps. She was afraid to look. All she knew was that it was silent for a long, long time.

After dinner, Chris and Phoebe went up to Chris's room to study. Chris sat at her desk while Phoebe curled up on the bed, looking over a stack of history notes.

"She makes me crazy, Pheeb."

"Don't think about it," Phoebe comforted her friend.

"Easy for you to say," Chris answered with a shake of her head.

Chris stared at the chemistry book in front of her. She hated these run-ins with Brenda. Why did this girl have to live in the same house with her, be part of her family? Maybe she had been wrong even to try and make things better. Maybe she shouldn't have listened to Ted in the first place.

And what about Ted? Why hadn't he called? If he was going to be angry at her, they might as well get it over with. Chris hated having things so unbalanced, so out of line.

Homework wasn't working for Phoebe, either. But it wasn't Brenda or Ted that was distracting her. It was a phrase of music, Woody's smile, Griffin's blue-gray eyes. When she remembered singing the duet, she felt a wonderful sensation deep within her, as if she were a soap bubble glistening in the sun, floating higher and higher into the air.

"Brenda. Ugh!"

Phoebe came back down to earth quickly. "Chris, you okay?"

Chris turned to her friend and smiled sadly. "Yeah. What a mess. I tried with Brenda. I really did."

"I know that, Chris. It's not your fault. She's just got problems. Don't blame yourself." She leaned over and patted Chris on the arm.

Chris touched Phoebe's hand. "Thanks, Pheeb. You're a great friend, you know that. Sorry you had to sit through that little scene."

"Aww," kidded Phoebe, "what are friends for." Both girls began to laugh softly.

There was a knock at the door. "Excuse me, girls. Telephone, Chris." Mrs. Austin's eyes looked sadder than ever.

"Thanks, Catherine." Chris waited for her stepmother to leave. "I hope Ted's not too mad at me," she whispered.

"Hello."

"Chris? Hi!!! I had to call and apologize for this afternoon. I really feel awful about it. Are you still mad at me?" It wasn't Ted. It was Laurie.

"Oh, hi, Laurie."

"Let's just forget the whole thing. Okay?" Laurie asked.

"Sure."

"Listen, I've decided to throw a big party and I want you to be the first one to know about it. It's two weeks from this Saturday. Can you come? I could still change the date if you can't."

"I'm sure I can come. Phoebe's over. Should I tell her too?"

64

"Of course. I expect her and Brad to be there. It's going to be a truly great party. I'm having it catered and we may even rent some rock videos to show on the big screen. I'm putting everything into making it the best."

"Sounds fun." Chris nodded. Laurie's parties over the summer had been great, so this one probably would be, too. Chris couldn't help wondering if the rock video theme had anything to do with Peter Lacey. "Laurie, how was the game? Who won?" Chris wanted to know what kind of mood Ted would be in.

"Ted hasn't called you yet? Oh, my God, it was incredible. You are not going to believe it!"

"What?"

"Well, first, thanks to your boyfriend, for the first time in six years, we beat those military creeps at Leesberg. Ted made a touchdown that was so exciting, I almost screamed my lungs out."

Chris smiled proudly. Now she wished she'd been there to see Ted play. She could imagine his strong, graceful body running faster than anyone else. Why had she let herself miss the game?

"That's great! Thanks, Laur, I'm going to get off so I can call him . . ."

"Wait! That's not all. It was a pretty rough game. There was a fight in the middle. It looked like John Marquette — you know that cute, hunky guy who's also a wrestler — anyway it looked like John started it, but it didn't take long before a dozen guys were on top of each other. Intense was the word for it."

"Did Ted get hurt?"

"Not a scratch. I saw him afterwards. You see — this is the best. After the game, our guys decided to celebrate. So — this was great — some guys from our team went back over to Leesberg and poured five gallons of pink paint all over that gross statue of General Lee that stands in front of their academy. And guess who poured the first can?"

"Who?"

"Your boyfriend!"

"Who?"

"Ted! The police almost caught them, but they got away in time. It was great, Ted's little MG speeding down Wisconsin Avenue with five football players hanging out. Chris, are you still there?"

"Yes. Um, Laurie, I have to get off now. Thanks for inviting me to your party."

"Sure. I just wish you could have been there. You would have loved it. Bye!"

Chris hung up the phone and stared in front of her. In an overly steady voice she relayed Laurie's news to Phoebe. Phoebe started to smile, but then she instantly read the furious expression on Chris's face.

"It's no big deal, Chris. It was just a dumb prank," Phoebe said, trying to smooth things over.

But Chris stopped listening. The tightness of her mouth was back, and her perfect features were hard and tense with rage. Phoebe had seen that look before. Chris's jaw would clench and her lips purse as if she wanted to hold back all the angry things she might say.

"If it was just a dumb prank, why were the police there? I do not believe it," Chris whispered fiercely. "Sometimes Ted is just plain stupid!"

"Chris, forget it. It's not that big a deal. Really," Phoebe pleaded.

"Not a big deal? Defacing a public monument? That's something a twelve-year-old delinquent would do. And then driving around in a tiny sportscar with five guys hanging out of it? Do you know how dangerous that is?"

"Come on, Chris. Laurie was probably exaggerating. I don't think five guys could fit in Ted's car."

Phoebe laughed a short, testy laugh, but Chris refused to relax and join in. Phoebe never knew what to do when her friend got like this. It was a stubborn, unbending side of Chris that she didn't understand.

"How would you feel if Brad did something like that? I'm serious. Tell me you'd just calmly sit there and think it was wonderful."

Phoebe couldn't even respond. The idea of Brad doing anything so careless, so wild, so spontaneous was beyond her imagination. It would never occur to Brad to pour pink paint on Robert E. Lee. She had the fleeting thought that she might like it if he *did* do something crazy like that every once in a while, but she didn't dare say it.

"Now I know why he hasn't called me. He knows how I feel about stuff like that."

"Look Chris, you're making too big a deal out of this." Phoebe took a quick peek at her watch. "Wow, it's already after eight. I'm sorry, but I gotta be home by eight-thirty. I still have to print some stuff for Brad tonight, and my dad needs the computer too." She began to gather up her history notes.

"Sure. I'll drive you. I'm sorry. You know how this kind of stuff makes me crazy."

As Phoebe stepped into the hall, Chris's step-mother came by carrying a basket of laundry into the master bedroom.

"Bye, Mrs. Austin. Thanks for a great dinner," Phoebe said.

Mrs. Austin smiled in appreciation, and Phoebe went downstairs to wait for Chris. She noticed Brenda sitting cross-legged on the couch with an open textbook in her lap. The pale upholstery made her hair look even darker. The two girls' eyes met for a moment.

"Hi," Phoebe said weakly. She didn't know what else to say. She barely knew Brenda, but she had heard so many personal things about her from Chris that it made her feel self-conscious.

Chris appeared in the entry hall, then stopped abruptly and looked at her stepsister.

"Oh, Chris," Brenda said in a voice that was cool and insinuating, "I just happened to pick up the phone when your friend Laurie called. I didn't mean to eavesdrop, but I couldn't help hearing about your boyfriend."

Chris was standing with one hand on the doorknob. She was frozen, suspended, waiting for Brenda to finish.

"That was a great prank," continued Brenda with a sarcastic edge. "Sounds like something one of *my* friends would have thought up."

Brenda gave her stepsister an innocent little smile.

Chapter
7

"I had a really good time at the game yesterday," cooed Laurie as Peter set up the next record. "I mean, it was really exciting, even if it was just a practice game. It's too bad you left so early. Did you hear what happened afterwards?"

Peter looked up from his control board for a split second, mumbled that he had heard all about painting General Lee, and went back to his beloved dials and meters. It was lunchtime and Peter was in the midst of his Kennedy High radio show. His face was tense with concentration as he posed his hand ready on the volume dial.

"Move aside, Laur," he whispered, watching the second hand on the overhead clock, "and don't talk to me while I'm on the air."

"Okay," Laurie said in her sexiest voice.

With a quick movement of his wrist, Peter

flipped the toggle switch and leaned into the microphone. "Okay, boys and girls, that was the latest from the High Tickets, rock 'n' roll's hottest new band. Next, we have a cut from the new Duran Duran. This one's just out. Remember, you heard it first on WKND." Peter's voice was rich and lively. In one motion, he cued the second turntable, spun around to adjust the volume controls, and flipped the toggle switch again.

Laurie watched Peter's intricate moves with fascination. There was nothing that appealed to her more than a boy who was really good at something. Peter's preoccupation with the station made the challenge even more enticing. Add to that the fact that supposedly no girl at Kennedy had succeeded in making him lose his heart, and Laurie was hooked. Not an easy one to catch, she thought, which was all the more reason to try.

Music filled the tiny studio until Peter twirled a dial to make it fade into the background. He opened the door and stuck his head out into the hall. "Janie, pull the new Michael Jackson for me, please." Peter himself preferred more offbeat groups, but he always played what his audience wanted to hear.

Janie Barstow, a tall, plain junior who was Peter's assistant, appeared two minutes later and handed the album through the doorway. "Here you go," she said in a very shy voice.

"Thanks." Peter took the album almost without looking at it and slid it out of its jacket onto the first turntable. "I'll be with you in a sec, Laurie," he said with a nod. After cuing the record, he whipped off his army surplus sweater

71

and tossed it over the back of his chair. Underneath was a short-sleeved black T-shirt. As soon as Duran Duran began to fade out, Peter brought up Michael Jackson, keeping his eyes glued to the volume dials.

"There. I can leave that on for two or three cuts." Peter wiped a bead of sweat from his forehead. "So, you're just going to talk on the radio for five minutes at the end of my half hour, right?"

Laurie smiled coyly.

"You know, I was thinking about this last night, Laur. I already announce school events and do interviews. Uh, are you sure Kennedy really needs another DJ?"

"Peter," Laurie soothed, "first, there could never be another WKND DJ besides you. I mean, you are the best, there's no question about that. And don't think this was my idea to take any of your time. It's just that the student council wanted to be sure that all the latest information on Kennedy's activities got publicized. Since I'm the activities officer, they asked me to do the radio rundown. If it were up to me, I'd just write a list for you to read every day, but they want to get the council involved," she continued in an innocent voice. "You know how it is." She leaned over the control board.

"Yeah, I know I'm a little overprotective about my station. I mean, it does belong to the whole school."

"Don't apologize, Peter. You have a right to be possessive of this station. You *are* WKND.

Everybody knows that." She looked straight at him with her big, almond-shaped eyes.

"Ahh." Peter laughed with an embarrassed wave of his hand. "All right. I guess I should start showing you how to use all this junk."

"Thank you, Peter." Laurie slithered closer to him.

"Okay. This button here is the first one to learn." Peter pointed to a push button on the far left corner of the control board. Underneath it were the words, "on air."

"You press this in when you want to talk over the radio. See that little light? That goes on when you're going out over the airwaves. If it's not on, the listeners can't hear you."

"Like now?" asked Laurie sweetly. She leaned down on the control board and rested her chin in her hands.

"Yeah. 'Cause obviously, Michael Jackson is on now. It's pretty simple." He moved a step away and explained the volume dials and use of the microphone. Laurie listened as if her life depended on it, commenting on how impressive and interesting it all was.

"Thanks, Peter. I think one or two more lessons and I'll be ready. It's different than I thought. You know, I've only been in my father's editing rooms. It's not the same at all."

Laurie's father had bought the most successful cable TV station in the D.C. area. That had been the reason the Benningtons had moved to Rose Hill from Los Angeles. As often as possible, Laurie reminded people that her father owned the station.

"Maybe sometime my dad will let me show you around his studios. You won't believe how amazing they are."

"Really? Wow. I've never been in a professional tv studio." Peter looked up excitedly.

Laurie smiled. At last, she had found her bait.

"You know my party? Maybe you could meet my dad then. He loves to help kids get their first jobs. Also, he has this state-of-the-art stereo that he won't let me touch. But I bet if he knew you worked for the radio station, he'd let you use it."

Peter looked up with delight, and Laurie knew she was on the right track.

"Peter, maybe you could do the records on my dad's stereo for the party. You know, be the DJ there, too."

There was a strategic pause. A look of anguish came over Laurie's face. "Oh, no, but yesterday you didn't know if you could come to my party or not. Well, maybe some other time. Maybe sometime when my dad's in town. He's always off in England or Japan or someplace."

"I can probably come to your party."

"You can? Are you sure?"

"I'm sure. Two weeks from tonight, right?"

"Right."

"I'll be there."

Laurie leaned back again the wall. How perfect it was all turning out! Her mind was already moving ahead to the party, but she made herself stop and concentrate on those last few moments she'd had with Peter.

"Well, great. That will be super. I'm sure my

dad will be really interested in meeting you."
Laurie smiled victoriously. "I guess you'd better
get back on the air. Thanks for showing me
around. Can I come in for another lesson sometime soon?" Laurie leaned casually against the
door, her jump suit showing off her perfect curve.

"Yeah. Just let Janie know ahead of time.
See you around."

Peter shut the heavy door and checked the
wall clock. He had only a few seconds before
Michael Jackson was finished. Laurie! What a
strange one. Hot and cold like a water faucet,
she was either gushing at people or telling them
where to get off. Peter didn't know if he could
handle her.

Still, she did seem to be interested in the
station, and she had an appeal that could make
her very popular as a social announcer. Plus,
there was no denying that she was absolutely
great-looking — not that looks came across on
the radio — but almost every guy at Kennedy
knew who she was. Peter knew they'd be imagining her fabulous face whenever they heard her
on the air. Add to that her ear for gossip, her
money, clothes, car, and her quick wit, and it
wasn't hard to see that Laurie would be a popular addition to WKND. Even if people didn't like
her, they'd like listening to her, so the number
of kids who tuned in to the station would rise.
It was that simple.

But then, Peter knew he was avoiding the real
issue. Laurie was obviously making a play for
him. Did he want to go out with her or not? On
that one, he still couldn't make up his mind.

Chris had been standing at her locker since the beginning of lunch period. At first, she'd used the excuse of sewing a ripped seam in the sleeve of her white cotton sweater. She'd actually noticed the rip that morning, but the other sweater she wanted to wear had been put accidentally in Brenda's room. Of course, Chris didn't want to have to see Brenda, so she ended up not changing and wearing the sweater with the rip in it.

It was stupid, but then, everything seemed stupid since she'd heard about what Ted had done at Leesberg. Pouring paint on General Lee — it sounded like a bunch of five-year-olds in a kindergarten class. And Brenda rubbing it in made it all the worse. OOOHHHHHHH! She could get mad all over again just thinking about it. She'd been trying to avoid Ted all day. And she hadn't called him last night either, because she was really mad and she knew they'd have a fight if they talked. But now that it was the middle of lunch hour and Chris still felt angry, she wondered just how long she could keep on avoiding him and whether she'd ever feel any less angry.

Chris grabbed what she needed for fifth period. She searched for a pencil in the checkered nylon sack that hung next to her picture of Sally Ride. She had to have a number-two pencil for fifth period algebra. Mr. McClure was fanatical about using a sharp number-two pencil. Then Chris remembered that she'd loaned it to Sasha that morning and Sasha had forgotten to return it.

That would mean she would have to go to the student store, which was bad because it was right off the quad. She was liable to bump into Ted.

Wow, what would she tell him? I'm avoiding you until I'm less mad at you? I love you, but you're so immature. Whatever made you do such a stupid, idiotic thing?

What really worried Chris was that Ted wouldn't take it seriously, he would think it didn't matter. What would she do if he laughed off something as big as this? If he just shrugged this off . . . well, then maybe they shouldn't be together.

That thought made Chris feel sick, and she slammed her locker shut. It couldn't be like that, she didn't want to break up. Phoebe had told her this morning that she would be making a big mistake if she broke up with Ted. Whatever weaknesses he might have, Phoebe said, there was nobody more perfect for Chris than Ted, and Chris knew that she was right. But on the other hand, Chris felt she had to draw a line. Her father had made her understand that.

Chris remembered how her father had taught her lessons. Like when she was younger, when her mom was still alive, she'd gone through a phase of being late all the time. Every Saturday morning, she would have a tennis lesson at Everdale Park, and then in the afternoon her dad would take her to a matinee. But Chris was always just a little bit late because she'd lose track of time down at the park. Her father finally told her that if she was late one more time, he'd stop taking her to the Saturday afternoon movies.

Chris was late the next time and, to her surprise, her father kept his word. They never went to a Saturday movie again. At first, that lesson had hurt a lot, but it had taught her never to be late for anything again. She had learned from the experience. That was what Ted needed now.

Chris walked down the hall quickly until she reached the student store. There was a line, and the girl behind the counter didn't seem to know how to use the cash register. Chris waited behind three other people while nervously glancing through the archway on her right that led out to the quad. She felt awful. As much as she didn't want to run into Ted, she also found herself missing him. How much longer could this go on? It was really confusing. She looked again toward the quad and blinked in the sunlight. She couldn't see the face of the person running toward her, but she certainly recognized his voice.

"Chris!" Ted called.

And then he was standing next to her and giving her a hug. People in line were looking at them. Chris stood very still and did not return Ted's gesture.

"I heard about the game," she said immediately.

Ted shook his head. Chris could tell that he was worried. The usual carefree expression was gone, and he didn't seem to stand quite as tall as he had yesterday.

"Well, we won," Ted said. He smiled weakly before going on. "But some other stuff happened."

"I heard about the other stuff, too," Chris said coldly.

"Yeah, I figured." Ted shrugged. "We got a little carried away." He started to laugh, but Chris's stern expression stopped him.

"Whose bright idea was it to have a painting party?"

Ted shifted. "Now that I think back about it, I'm not really sure. It all started because there was this fight on the field."

Chris sighed. Ted really hated fighting. He was so quick and strong and passionate, most people assumed that he'd be the first to throw a punch. But it wasn't true. Ted was the first person to try to *stop* a fight. He had the utmost contempt for those who somehow thought that fighting was brave or macho.

"Anyway," Ted continued, "this stupid fight broke out between the linemen from Leesberg and Marquette."

"Marquette? You mean John Marquette?" Chris asked. "I should have known. He's such a bully."

"Wait a second," Ted cautioned, "that's what I'm trying to explain. He didn't start it."

"Then who did?"

"One of the guys from Leesberg. We were beating them really badly and they just couldn't take it, so they started a fight. Marquette just fought back, until I grabbed him and the whole thing died down."

Chris suddenly stopped being so angry at Ted and began to feel just a little bit proud.

"Next, please," the girl at the cash register said to Chris. She quickly bought her pencil, and she and Ted started to walk away. They found a table on the edge of the quad and sat down. Chris tried to hide the tiny smile that was inching onto her face.

"Uh-oh, I saw that," Ted teased. "Watch out. I think you may be starting to forgive me."

"Okay." Chris put on her most serious expression. "You stopped a fight. That's great. Now, what happened to change you from this noble fight-stopper to a malicious paint-thrower?"

"Chris, you weren't there," Ted pleaded. "Those guys from Leesberg pulled some really dirty stuff. They deserved it."

"They deserved it? The two or three jerks on the Leesberg football team made up for wrecking something that belongs to the whole academy?"

Ted gave her an innocent smile.

"Ted, I'm serious! I also heard that you were driving like a wreckless maniac."

"Who told you that?"

"Laurie. She said guys were hanging out of your car."

Ted scowled, "Well, we had to get away pretty fast. It wasn't dangerous or anything. Honest."

"Kids get killed that way, Ted. Face it, you really acted like a jerk."

The words stung Ted. Chris could see it in his face. They should sting, she thought. Ted had to know that there were certain limits.

"Well, listen," Ted went on, "if you'd been at the game like I wanted you to, none of this would have happened. If I'd known you were waiting in the stands, I never would even have thought of it."

"Thought of it! Thought of it!!! Are you telling me that this whole thing was your idea?" Chris was stunned.

Ted looked caught. "Well, sort of. I mean, we all kind of thought of it together . . . um, I don't know."

"Oh, yes, you do know," Chris pushed on.

"Come on, Chris. I don't need this right now. Today has not been one of my more fun days. Did you ever stop to think why I didn't call you last night?"

"I just figured you were too embarrassed," Chris said angrily.

"Did you ever think that you might not be the only person who wants to punish me for my terrible crime?" Ted's voice was getting hard and sarcastic.

"What do you mean?"

"The reason that I didn't call you last night was because I was just a little bummed out after I got a call from the coach."

Chris froze. "The coach? What did he say?"

"Oh, not much. Just that what we did was very unsportsmanlike and that the head guy at Leesberg had called him." Ted stared off disgustedly. "And that I'm benched."

"Oh, no."

"I'm not starting in the next game. He was going to punish us even worse, but since those cadets played so dirty . . . anyway, I can keep coming to practice."

"Ted, I'm sorry," said Chris softly. "At least he didn't kick you off the team."

"Nah. I don't think he really wanted to punish us at all," he said with a little too much confidence. "He just had to do something to show that head guy at Leesberg. I'm sure he'll act real tough with us and all, but deep down, I think he's kind of proud of us."

"I hardly think that, Ted."

"Well, I do. Those cadets pulled some real low junk on us. We deserved to show them what we thought of them."

"Ted."

"I don't care. It's better than fighting. They can wash the paint off . . . I think. If some other team pulls that kind of stuff, I'll do it again."

"Ted" — Chris was getting angry again — "I can't believe I'm hearing you say this. You just did something incredibly stupid, and now you're telling me you'd do it again! What is wrong with you?"

"What's wrong with you, Chris? Why don't you support me when something goes wrong, instead of attacking me. You're supposed to be my girlfriend. So how come you're worse about this than the coach?" Ted 's voice was rising.

"Well, maybe I shouldn't be your girlfriend. We obviously feel so differently about things." As soon as the words were out of her mouth, Chris felt sick again.

"Well, maybe you shouldn't be. I'm beginning to think that's what the problem is here."

Chris's light complexion began to turn deep red. "Look, Ted, you messed up! Don't try and blame it on me!"

Ted stood up and grabbed his notebook. "I wouldn't dream of blaming anything on you, Miss Perfect! I'm sure you never do anything wrong. Well, listen, Chris, I don't need you to remind me of all the ways I've messed up, okay? I think we'll both be better off if we just go our separate ways, don't you?"

Chris stood up with a jolt. "I certainly do. You just go ahead and paint more statues, or whatever it is that you want to do, and don't worry about me. Because I won't be around to worry about you."

"Well, that's just fine with me!"

"Good!"

Their voices were topped by the bell. Glaring at each other, Chris and Ted turned abruptly away and stormed off in opposite directions. Chris knew after a few steps that she was headed in the wrong direction if she were going to go to her class, but she wasn't about to turn around now. Geraldine Gomez, from honor society, was staring at her, but Chris didn't care. Chris didn't even bother to say hello or stare back. She couldn't have if she'd wanted to. Her voice was gone, her heart was pounding, she felt hot all over, and the tears were starting to turn everything into one big blur.

Chapter
8

Phoebe and Chris spent most of the weekend together. Phoebe didn't want her friend to have to be alone after her breakup with Ted, and the last place Chris wanted to be was at home with Brenda. Brad hadn't minded including Chris in their Saturday date to see *Nerd Heaven,* a new movie at the Rose Hill shopping mall. The movie was as silly and slapsticky as Phoebe had expected, but unfortunately there was one serious love scene between the heroine and a young actor who slightly resembled Ted. Halfway through the scene, Chris ran up the aisle. Phoebe spent the rest of the movie with her in the bathroom. Afterwards, Brad had assured them that they hadn't missed much.

Besides the duty of friendship, which Phoebe took very seriously, there was another reason why Phoebe welcomed Chris's company on her date with Brad. She had not yet told Brad about auditioning for the Follies. After all, she wouldn't know for sure that she had been picked until Woody posted the list on Monday. There was no point in discussing something that might not even happen. In any case, Chris's presence had prevented any serious talk.

Actually, it had been a warm and comfortable weekend for Phoebe and Brad. Phoebe supposed that Chris and Ted's breakup had made her and Brad realize how lucky they were to still be a couple. Two years and they still loved each other, still had a good time together, still almost never fought. It was so easy to take each other for granted and forget what a rare thing it was to stay with someone for a long time.

By the time Monday morning arrived and Phoebe nervously cut across the quad to see if her name was on Woody's list, she had convinced herself that Brad wouldn't mind even if she were in the Follies. Well, he'd probably mind at first, but he wouldn't make a big deal out of it. So what if he thought the Follies were dumb, it was her up there singing, not him.

The quad was wet and slippery from a heavy rain the night before, and Phoebe could feel the cool dampness through the soles of her flat shoes. There was a cold edge in the early morning air, reminding her that the mild weather would soon give way to the wet Maryland winter. Zipping her red shiny rain slicker, Phoebe patted her stomach to ease the butterflies that were rising as she neared the Little Theater. What if her name wasn't on the list? Well, that would certainly solve the problem with Brad. Yet Phoebe knew that her disappointment at not being selected for the Follies would be worse than any run-in with her boyfriend.

She could see the list taped onto the Little Theater door from the middle of the quad. Four or five kids were huddled around it, and something about them made Phoebe stop. For a moment Phoebe thought one of them was Griffin. Then she realized the boy looked nothing like Griffin. He did, though, look excited at obviously having made the show. Singer Jane McGraw looked less happy as she slowly walked away. When Phoebe passed her, Jane looked down at the grass with a grim expression.

Phoebe held her breath as she climbed the old wooden steps to the theater. Closing her eyes, she made a silent plea for success and waited for two of the members of Blue Moon to move aside so she could read the names. When she opened her eyes again, the list was hanging clearly in front of her. Trying to stay calm, Phoebe skimmed a third of the way down the piece of paper.

Suddenly, she felt a burst of joy. There it was. Her name, Phoebe Hall, written plainly for everyone to see. She clapped her hands together once and bounced up and down on her heels. This was great! She had made it! Before she realized what she was doing, Phoebe found herself scanning the list for another name. Sure enough, it was also there. Another third of the way down the alphabetical list from her name was Griffin Neill's.

Phoebe was vaguely aware that someone near her was clapping his hands.

"Yaayyy, Phoeberooni! Congrats." Woody was

standing at the bottom of the stairs, applauding her. "I'm so glad you decided to be in the show. You were great at the audition, absolutely great. It took all my self-control not to call you over the weekend and let you know."

Phoebe hopped down the steps to join Woody, and he led her away from the small crowd by the theater. He was smiling his bright, toothy smile and had his thumb hooked in his red suspenders. "I can't stand too close to the list or I might get belted by some poor rejected artist." He laughed, his big eyes crinkling around the corners.

Phoebe gave him a quick, friendly hug. "Woody, thanks. I'm really excited that you picked me."

Woody turned his head, but Phoebe could see that he was blushing. "Well, Pheeb, you'd better be excited. Everybody better be. We have only two weeks to put this thing together, so we're going to have to work our buns off. The performance date is October twentieth. First rehearsal is today after school."

"Okay," Phoebe answered happily. "What song do you think I should sing?" Phoebe knew that Woody often switched things around, sometimes surprising kids with what he asked them to perform.

"I thought you and Griffin should do the same song you did for the audition. It was truly great."

Phoebe smiled. For some reason, she'd hoped Woody would say that.

"So, Chris, are you going to Laurie's party?" Peter asked as he munched on a crisp apple.

"I guess," answered Chris moodily. "I told her I would." She looked around the quad for Ted, but he was obviously staying out of her way. She hadn't seen or spoken to him since they'd broken up.

"Yeah. I'm going to do the records, so that should be pretty fun," Peter continued.

Sasha looked up from her avocado sandwich. "Why aren't you on the radio today, Peter?"

"Some kind of problem with the transmitter. It'll be fixed in a couple days. It's kinda nice to be out here with everybody for a change."

"I miss the music," commented Woody with a mouth full of potato chips. "I'm so used to your show that sometimes I don't even notice it, but now that it's gone I miss it."

"Thanks a lot, Webster. What a compliment. I love your little skits, too." Peter knew that Woody liked his projects to be called "shows," not "skits." They both laughed good-naturedly.

Phoebe dug into her carton of cottage cheese and wondered where Brad was. By ten minutes into the lunch period, he was usually there. Phoebe looked around at her friends relaxing over lunch. Sasha sat cross-legged on the bench, her long, dark hair waving in the breeze; Peter was sprawled on the grass, and Woody leaned against a cherry tree. A few other friends sat in a loose circle on the ground. They were all eating hungrily except Chris, who picked gloomily at the salad in her plastic container.

The main topic of conversation was Laurie's party. Since Laurie was taking a make-up test, it was a good time to discuss it. They had all promised to go and predicted that it would be quite a bash.

"That party of hers over the summer was pretty amazing. I'd never have the nerve to move to a new town and invite all these kids I didn't know," marveled Sasha. "And then the food. I'd never seen so much Mexican food in my life."

"Yeah, it was great," joked Woody. "Phoebe got sick from eating too much. Brad wouldn't get out of the pool until he finally beat Ted in water basketball. Sasha, you got a second-degree sunburn and made us all sign that petition to save the seals in — where was it — Alaska?"

"Canada," corrected Sasha.

"Okay, Canada," Woody said, "and I spent the whole time chasing that knockout cousin of Laurie's from California. Then at the end of the party, she told me she already had a boyfriend and she just wanted to be friends."

"Gee, I'm sorry I missed it. Sounds like it was a great party," Peter joked, and tossed his apple core and watched it sail into the trash can.

"Well, from what I hear, Laurie's really going all out on this one." Woody turned around and jump-shot his crumpled-up brown bag. It also went into the basket.

"Laurie seems to go all out in everything she does," Peter said, a little glumly. "She can really come on strong."

"Yeah, I know what you mean," Woody said. "She does kind of bowl you over sometimes."

"Well, she's new," Sasha said. "Maybe that's

just her way of trying to meet people." Sasha always gave new kids the benefit of the doubt.

"Sometimes she's a little . . . weird," Phoebe said, remembering the incident between Laurie and Brenda. She glanced over at Chris, who obviously wasn't listening. "But you're right, Sasha. We don't know her very well. I'm sure she's just a little nervous about being new here. She can be really nice."

"Hey, Pheeb," Woody said, "I think somebody's trying to get your attention."

Phoebe looked over and spotted Brad coming out of the main office building. He was waving his hands over his head as though he were really excited about something. It looked like he was gesturing for her to come over and join him. Phoebe quickly got up and, dodging different groups of kids who were sitting on the grass, jogged across the lawn to where Brad stood.

When Phoebe got closer, she saw an expression of pure joy on Brad's face. She hadn't seen him that happy in ages. Whatever it was that had happened, it was obviously good. Feeling a burst of warmth, Phoebe ran the last few feet.

"Phoebe! Phoebe, it's great!" Brad soon had her in his arms and was lifting her straight up toward the sky. Phoebe looked down at his bright, exuberant face. "I'm so psyched," he said, setting Phoebe's feet on the ground again.

"You are?"

"Yeah." Brad gave her a silly grin and another big hug, his brown eyes sparkling.

"Brad! What's up?" Phoebe demanded happily, "tell me!"

He stepped back and tried to look cool. "Your boyfriend just happens to have taken his first step on the way to Princeton University.

"You got your interview?"

"Today. Mom left a message at the office for me. I just called her. The letter from Princeton came this morning with my interview time. Not only that, but the letter said they've received my school records already and that I should consider applying for early admission. Early admission! You know what that means?"

"What?"

"That they're really interested in me. Oh, Pheeb, I'm flying, I'm so excited."

Phoebe grabbed Brad around the neck and kissed him hard on the mouth, ignoring the many kids who were standing nearby. "Brad, that's great! I'm so proud of you. I told you they'd want you, didn't I? They'd be fools not to take you."

"Well, I haven't gotten in yet, but — Whew, what a relief to have that interview set."

It was a very good day, Phoebe thought, for her and for Brad.

"Mom called my uncle in New Jersey first thing, and it's all set up for us to stay the night. The interview is at eight on Saturday morning, so we'll go up there Friday after school. We're supposed to have dinner that night with my uncle's friend — you know, the one who was premed at Princeton — and then we can be back in time for Laurie's party on Saturday night."

Phoebe stopped. "Wait, Brad. What's the date of the interview?"

91

"It's at eight A.M., October twenty-first, so that's two weeks from this Saturday."

Suddenly, the day wasn't quite so terrific anymore. The Follies performance was the night of October the twentieth. How could she be singing in the Little Theater and having dinner with Brad's uncle's friend at the same time? Phoebe felt like she was falling, going down faster and faster, until soon, she wouldn't be able to breathe. It was finally time to tell Brad about the Follies.

"Brad," Phoebe said in a quiet voice.

"What is it, Pheeb? What's wrong?"

"I can't go to Princeton with you on the night of October twentieth." Phoebe couldn't look at him.

"Why not? My mom will call your mom and tell her it's okay. I mean, it's not like we're staying in a motel or something. It's my uncle's huge house. She'll understand."

"That's not it. I told Woody that I'd be in the Follies, and the performance is that night."

Brad just stood there for a minute and looked at Phoebe as though she were speaking Swahili. "What?"

Phoebe felt her legs turning to rubber and sat down on a nearby bench. "I'm going to sing in the Follies, and the show is on the same night you want to go up to Princeton."

Collapsing slowly into the seat next to her, Brad shook his head. "I didn't even know you tried out. I don't get it. Just tell Woody you can't be in it."

"Brad, you don't understand. The auditions

last week were really terrific, and Woody picked me for the show. I told him I'd be in it."

"You knew about this last week and you didn't tell me? What is this with you and Woody, anyway?"

"I didn't tell you because I didn't know for sure and. . . ."

"And you knew this might happen. I can't believe you would do that instead of going to Princeton with me. This is the most important thing I'm going to do all year."

"The Follies may be the most important thing *I* do all year. Did you ever stop to think of it that way?"

Brad brought his voice down, aware that kids might be watching them. "If you like Woody so much, why don't you just break up with me and start going out with him? I have a feeling that's just what he wants."

"This has nothing to do with Woody!" Phoebe almost yelled. Brad motioned for her to speak more softly, but she ignored him. "This has to do with me. I'm sorry that I can't go to Princeton with you. I want to go. I think it's great that they're so interested in you. But Brad, I have to do something that makes me feel like I'm somebody special, like I'm worthwhile too. Being part of the Follies makes me feel that way. You may think it's really dumb, but I don't."

The last was said very loudly, and Phoebe could feel the tears starting to catch in her voice. She knew she would start crying soon. Quickly, she grabbed her shoulder bag and walked into a more secluded area just outside the counselor's office. Brad followed.

Phoebe leaned with her back to the wall, her fists pushed into the pockets of her overalls. Much as she tried to stop them, her tears started to flow. Ugh! Why couldn't she ever have an argument or even an emotional discussion without breaking into tears. Whenever anybody got even a little annoyed at her, she immediately got that awful lump in her throat and started to cry.

Facing the wall, leaning on one arm, Brad stood next to her.

"Brad, I'm really sorry," Phoebe said finally.

"I know," he responded.

"Maybe we can still work it out."

"How?"

"The important part is the interview, right?" Brad looked at her.

"Why don't I come up early on the train Saturday morning. I don't need to be there the night before. What time is the appointment?" Phoebe sniffed.

Brad threw his head back. "Eight A.M., which means you wouldn't have to take a train before say two or three o'clock in the morning."

Phoebe flinched. "There might be a train that's early enough. I mean, if it's really important. . . ."

"Forget it, Phoebe. Just forget it. I can go alone."

Phoebe felt like she wanted to scream. Her head was beginning to ache and the back of her neck was rock hard. She just wanted all this awfulness to go away and for everything to be pleasant again.

"Brad, I am really sorry. I had no idea the Follies and your interview would be at the same time. Honest. I don't know. Maybe I should tell Woody I can't do the show. We haven't started rehearsing yet. . . ."

Brad rubbed his forehead with the palm of his hand. "No, it's okay. Do the show."

Brad kicked an empty paper bag that was lying in the middle of the hall.

"Brad, I'm sorry."

"I know."

Phoebe stood up straight and wiped the mascara from her cheeks. "I have the papers for your student council meeting this afternoon. I left them in my book bag with the crowd," she said.

"Oh. Yeah. Thanks."

"Do you want me to get them for you?"

"Sure. I guess I'll walk back over there with you. Just give me a sec to cool out, okay?"

Phoebe nodded and took out the antique compact with the picture of the red-haired woman on it. Peering into the little mirror, she saw that her face was marked with tears and her eyes were red. She rubbed a few smudges of makeup from under her eyes and took a deep breath. Brad was standing looking at her with his hands on his hips.

"Let's go," he said evenly.

"Okay."

Brad and Phoebe walked back into the quad for the last few minutes of lunch. No one noticed anything strange about the way they were acting. That is, no one but Chris, who realized right off that something was wrong between Brad and Phoebe. It was the first time she had ever seen them walk across the lawn together not holding hands.

Chapter
9

"Karen, can you have John bring up light number eleven?"

"Okay, Woody."

"And not so green. Everything I'm seeing today looks green."

Everything Phoebe was seeing looked gray, or at least mushy and brown and indistinct. And everything inside . . . well, it wasn't fizzy or carbonated anymore, but it was soft and tender and it hurt. Sitting in a dark corner of the Little Theater, she wondered if she weren't a living version of the Pillsbury Doughboy. All the people she cared about most were pulling and poking her from different directions, and she felt very vulnerable.

Take Woody, for instance. He was so sweet and so talented. But he kept giving her those big moon eyes. After the big fight about Princeton, he had heard rumors that she and Brad were having their little troubles — Laurie Bennington had seen to that.

Of course, the rumors were exaggerated, and Phoebe just wasn't sure how to react to Woody. This morning, she'd tried to ignore him when he'd waited around her locker for her. As she'd gotten her books, he'd hung onto the door, looking like a big flag flapping on a flagpole. She'd worried that Brad was going to see him there and take it the wrong way.

Then there was Chris. Chris! How could somebody who had so much going for her get so hysterical? She and Ted were not speaking to each other. When they walked past each other in the hallways it was like they didn't even know each other. It was totally ridiculous, too, because the more Chris tried to act tough and hard and uncaring, the more Phoebe was having to spend time passing her tissues in the girls' bathroom to wipe away her tears. Between boxes, she kept asking Phoebe if she was doing the right thing. But Phoebe knew the worst was yet to come. Laurie had been spreading rumors again — this time about Ted. He had been seen with a certain little French girl who was new at Kennedy, the daughter of a diplomat. When Chris found out about that, fireworks were going to go off.

Then, of course, there was Brad. They had gotten over their fight about Princeton, but there was tension about everything they did together. Brad also had so much work to get done for his interview. He needed her help, and after the way she had let him down about missing the trip to Princeton, there was no way she could refuse. So now she had to help Brad, go to rehearsals, get to class, and somehow manage to do her homework too — to say nothing of eating, sleeping, changing her clothes, and making her bed.

But Phoebe had to admit that rehearsals were never a chore. Listening to the echo of excited voices gave her a lift and a thrill. She loved just being in the old building. Dusty and damp, the chapel smelled like the tool shed behind Phoebe's family's first house in Rose Hill. Phoebe had loved playing make-believe in that shed as a little girl just as she loved the messy, high-ceilinged interior of the theater.

Randy Nakamora sat down at the piano which stood on one side of the stage. A moment later, five kids swarmed around him and began to sing a five-part version of "Memory" from the musical, *Cats*. Phoebe started to hum along and waved to Woody, who was still checking the lights and conferring with Miss Weidemann, the drama teacher and adviser for the talent show.

"How have you been," asked a clear, melodic voice.

Phoebe turned and felt her cheeks flush. Griffin Neill was leaning against the back of the seat next to her. He looked at her over his shoulder with a wide-eyed smile. His gray hooded sweatshirt was unzipped, revealing a T-shirt with a Baltimore Orioles logo.

"Oh, okay," Phoebe said shyly. The more time she spent with Griffin, the more she liked him. She always looked forward to talking to him and singing with him at rehearsals; but often, when he was close to her, she felt oddly flustered and nervous. Griffin was always friendly, but lately he seemed just a little distant. Phoebe couldn't figure out why. Maybe it had something to do with her mention of Brad, during their first rehearsal together.

She thought back to that moment. Griffin had run up to her as soon as she'd walked into the theater.

"I can't wait to sing with you again!" he'd said excitedly. "We make a good team. Woody decided to let me do two acting sketches, too. I've almost got my lines down."

"Really? You mean you're an actor, too?" Phoebe had looked up at him in surprise.

"Singing is the same thing, it's just acting to music." Phoebe had nodded.

Griffin had taken Phoebe by the arm and guided her over to two seats in the back of the theater. They'd sat down close together, his shoulder resting against hers, and he'd leaned in close. "I saw you on the quad today during lunch. Is that your boyfriend?"

Phoebe had wrinkled her forehead, taken aback for a moment. Was it possible that Griffin didn't know she and Brad were a couple? Phoebe realized they weren't like Prince Charles and Diana, but still, most kids on campus knew about them. She'd nodded yes, Brad was her boyfriend.

"Isn't he some student body bigwig or something?"

"Student body president."

"Right. Brad something."

"Brad Davidson. I can't believe you don't know him. What year are you?" Phoebe had wondered again why she'd never noticed Griffin around school before.

"Senior. I just never pay attention to that stuff, I guess. I'm usually thinking about other things." Griffin had shrugged. "Have you been going with him for a long time?"

"Two years."

"Hmmm. Sounds serious to me." As Griffin had smiled, Phoebe had noticed two small dimples in his cheeks.

Phoebe's memory of that first rehearsal was interrupted as Woody called for the group's attention. "I better get up front." Now Griffin gave Phoebe a playful look. "My skits are two of the first acts to be rehearsed." He moved down the aisle and took a seat in the front of the theater. Phoebe found herself staring as dancer Joan Lavelle quickly came over and sat next to him. As Joan sat down, Griffin looked back at Phoebe. Instantly, Phoebe switched her gaze to Woody and pretended she had not been watching Griffin. It was then that she noticed her heart beating just a little bit faster.

Chris decided to go to the library to study after school, instead of going home where she might have to talk to Brenda or explain her sad eyes to her stepmother. Actually, she had gone over to the football field first, just to get a glimpse of Ted. It was dumb, she knew, and something she wouldn't admit to anyone, but she just wanted to look at him. Thank goodness he hadn't seen her or she didn't know what she would have done. He had been scrimmaging with the other guys and she had picked him out immediately by the number on his practice uniform. Then Coach Briggs had called him over and he had jogged over to the older man with his forceful, graceful run. When Ted had whipped off his helmet, Chris had almost started to cry.

There she had been, hiding behind a stocky old tree, watching Ted stand there with his helmet tucked under his arm listening attentively to his coach's advice. His white practice pants were covered with dirt, and his shirt, cut off at midchest, exposed his slim, muscled stomach. Looking at the ground, he had nodded slowly before pulling his helmet on and racing back to join the others. He hadn't looked her way.

Now, in the library, Chris looked up from her copy of *Great Expectations*. She had just read the scene where Pip finds old Miss Havisham in the attic. In the book, the boy finally goes upstairs and finds this crazy old lady still wearing her wedding dress from a marriage that hadn't taken place thirty years earlier. Rats are crawling in and out of the wedding cake.

Reading the scene made Chris shudder, and she had to close the book. Sometimes she felt like that, not old and crazy, but alone up there in the attic. She had felt like that ever since her mother had died, really since she'd first found out that her mother was sick. Every so often, it all came back to her: the silent days at home when her mom would be sleeping off the effects of the drugs that were supposed to be making her better, the starched, unnatural smell of the hospital; but most of all, her mom's soft, loving smile peeking through her ravaged face. And then one day, it was over. After all the near-misses and the treatments and the operations, her mom finally didn't come home.

Chris never talked about her mom any more. Even her father rarely mentioned her. As popular as Chris was, she didn't really share herself with many people. Phoebe was the only one of her girlfriends who had ever heard anything about her mother's illness. And of course she had told Ted everything.

From the very beginning, there was something different about Ted, something that made her want to share the most hidden parts of herself. He had no fear. There was nothing that was too painful or too private as far as he was concerned. Chris had to admit it, Ted was the first boy she had ever loved. And now, just like with her mother, it was over.

As she walked slowly home from the library, Chris missed Phoebe, too. With Phoebe busy at rehearsal, Chris was without the one person she could always count on for friendship and support. Like when she had burst into tears during that dumb movie over the weekend. Phoebe had sat with her in the bathroom, told Chris that she had to follow her own conscience, and cheered her up with popcorn and cherry bonbons. Phoebe was a true friend. But with the Follies getting closer, Phoebe was very busy and had less time for her.

As Chris rounded the corner of her street, she saw Catherine's beige Toyota pull in ahead of her and park in the driveway. Catherine and

Brenda climbed out, each carrying paper bags of different colors and sizes. Chris had forgotten they'd planned to go shopping. Catherine had invited Chris to join them in an attempt to patch things up between the two girls, but Chris had declined. Brenda was the last person she wanted to be with. Her stepsister was just one more problem she wanted to avoid thinking about.

Loaded down with packages, Brenda and Catherine went on into the house. Chris followed a minute later.

"Hi, dear." Catherine smiled. She and Brenda were sitting in the living room looking over the results of their shopping spree. "You should have come with us. They had the cutest things on sale at the mall. Brenda, show Chris the outfit you got at The Limited."

Brenda gave her stepsister a cold stare but did silently lift up her new pair of baggy dyed jeans and a funky striped blazer. The outfit was stylish and offbeat.

"Very nice," Chris mumbled and started to head for the stairs.

"Chris" — Catherine's rosy voice stopped her — "why don't you slip the jacket on. It's one of those oversized cuts, so I think it would fit you too. Maybe Brenda would let you borrow it once in a while."

Chris glared at Brenda, but her stepsister was poking in another sack. Please, Catherine, thought Chris, don't push it. As it turned out, the jacket was not at all in line with Chris's classic taste. Besides, she and Brenda were never likely to be the kind of sisters to swap clothes.

"That's okay, Catherine. I have my Ralph Lauren blazer that Daddy got me last year. It's kind of the same color, and it's my favorite." Chris paused before making another effort to leave the room. "But thanks, Brenda," she added stiffly.

Brenda and Catherine looked at each other. Chris began to wonder if the shopping trip hadn't included some mother-daughter soul-searching.

"If you decide you do want to borrow it, just ask me," Brenda said, trying hard to sound off-handed, as she ripped the price tag off of a pair of thick red socks.

Chris's mouth almost fell open. Was this Brenda, her stepsister, offering to share her brand new blazer with her? Chris began to wonder what kinds of arguments and threats had taken place in the dressing rooms of Rose Hill mall.

Catherine walked over to Brenda and put her arm around her warmly. "I don't know about you two, but I'm starving, and I'm sure your father will be too when he gets home. Brenda, why don't you hang everything up and set the table." Catherine gave her daughter a glowing smile and smoothed the side of Brenda's long, layered hair. Brenda smiled back at her mother, and Catherine padded off into the kitchen.

Chris felt very strange. Now that Catherine was gone, Brenda continued to absorb herself with tags and sales slips, avoiding any more words with her stepsister. It was obvious that Catherine was trying to make a clean start between the sisters. But that didn't make Chris feel better; if anything, this awkward attempt only made her feel worse, more alone, more left out. Seeing Catherine and Brenda so close made her miss her own mother all the more. That ache of loneliness Chris was working so hard to contain began to rise and swell.

The phone rang with a loud annoying brrinnggg. Brenda glanced at Chris and leaned over to pick it up.

"Hello," Brenda answered hoarsely. "Yeah, she's right here. Hold on." Brenda held out the phone. "It's for you."

Chris started to reach across the coffee table.

"It's your boyfriend."

Chris stopped, then took a deep breath. "Tell him I don't want to talk to him," she said finally. "And tell him not to bother to call again."

"Okay."

A few seconds later, the conversation was over, and Brenda hung up the phone. Chris didn't know where she was for a moment, and then she heard Brenda's voice, now very soft.

"I think he really wanted to talk to you. I mean I got . . ."

Chris was walking out of the living room even before Brenda could finish her sentence.

Chapter 10

"**B**rad's pretending that he's forgiven me, but it's like having a relationship on eggshells," Phoebe told Chris after school on Friday.

Chris sat with her back against a tree and her arms around her bare knees. It was one of the last days that she would be able to wear her favorite khaki walking shorts. Soon, it would be too cold. She slipped off her Topsider and dangled her argyled foot in a pile of leaves. All things come to an end, she thought.

"Have you talked to Ted at all?" asked Phoebe delicately. Chris looked up, her eyes as colorful as her royal blue turtleneck. Phoebe wondered if sadness could make your eyes look bluer.

"I've seen him a few times in the halls, but I couldn't tell if he saw me or not. I told him not to call me anymore, and that's just what he's done. I don't know. After what I saw this morning, I don't think he's suffering too much."

"Why do you say that?"

"Come on, Phoebe. Everybody's seen him with that little freshman girl. And if that wasn't bad enough, Laurie told anybody who didn't. I hear she's from France or something."

Phoebe flinched, so Chris had found out. It had been only a matter of time, the way Laurie had been talking about it. "Well, her name is Danielle DuClos," Phoebe volunteered, glad finally to get it out in the open. "I guess her father is a diplomat, so she's here for a year."

"A freshman! What's Ted doing, robbing the cradle?" Chris angrily pushed a strand of blond hair away from her mouth.

With a shrug, Phoebe refrained from reminding Chris that Danielle was gorgeous and that all the boys were supposedly in love with her thick French accent.

"Chris, she was simply in the car with him, that's no big deal. He probably just gave her a ride to school."

"Sure," Chris agreed sarcastically.

Phoebe was glad she never had to worry about other girls and Brad. Not that other girls weren't interested in him. But Brad was so loyal and steady he didn't notice them. Phoebe kept telling herself how lucky she was and that she shouldn't take his loyalty for granted.

"I have to just accept that it's over with Ted," Chris said, with more courage than Phoebe ever thought she herself could summon. "It's stupid for me to be so upset. We broke up. It happens every day. You must be really sick of hearing about it. I need to stop being so boring and go on with my life, right?"

"I think you have a right to be upset," Phoebe reasoned, "and I don't mind talking about it. That's what friends are for."

"Well, I think I'm being incredibly boring and we should talk about something else." Chris sat up straighter. "How are the Follies?"

"Coming along." Phoebe smiled. "Woody gave me another song, a solo. So now I have the duet of 'Sweet Beginnings' with Griffin Neill and 'Maybe This Time' — you know, from *Cabaret* — and that's all by myself."

"Phoebe, that's great. I really wish I could figure out who this Griffin guy is. Anyway, I can't wait to hear you sing again. I knew you'll be terrific."

Phoebe shook her head with a meek smile. She wasn't so sure that she was going to be any good at all. Still, it had been one of the best weeks in her life. Every day, she waited for seventh period to be over. It was torture watching the hand on the clock click forward at such an agonizingly slow pace. But when the bell finally rang, she felt such a rush of joy and anticipation that it made up for every tedious second of computer math. That bell meant it was time to race across the quad and join Woody and the others for rehearsal.

That old fizzy feeling had begun to ease up. She still got it when she thought about how she had messed up with Brad, but even that bothered her less and less as each day went by. All she knew was that when she was in the theater, she didn't worry about what had happened in her last class, or what might happen tomorrow, or who she was or why she was there. She just worked on her songs, helped others work on theirs, and felt alive and content. There was plenty of time to be nervous about Brad or the performance next week, but for now, she was just enjoying being a part of something special.

Phoebe looked up and saw a lanky male figure jogging towards them. He was coming from the direction of the theater. Phoebe knew instantly who it was — Griffin Neill.

"Oh, who's that?" Chris said in a conspiratorial whisper, straightening up as Griffin neared.

Phoebe sat up herself, trying not to seem curious about Griffin or interested in him. She pretended she hadn't noticed him. She felt strange around him, sort of shy, and awkward. He acted a little strange around her, too. At rehearsal, he was polite to her, almost distant. And yet, in those moments when they sang their duet together, she always felt that his eyes cut through to her very soul. It was as if there was some secret kind of communication between them that only surfaced at a few special times.

"Hi," Griffin panted.

"Hi," Phoebe said as casually as she could.

"It's nice out here, huh?"

He was doing it again. Maybe he couldn't help it. He was looking right into Phoebe's eyes and it was like X rays or lasers. Phoebe was afraid she was going to blush.

"We're going to start in a few minutes," Griffin

said finally. With a friendly nod to Chris, he turned and ran back across the lawn.

"Wow, he's cute," Chris uttered without the slightest hesitation. "What does he do in the show?"

"We sing a duet, and he acts." Phoebe tried to be cool.

"So that's Griffin Neill. Why didn't you tell me he was so good-looking? You know, I've almost never seen a guy look at a girl like that. It was as if electric currents were coming out of his eyes."

Phoebe laughed self-consciously. "It's just that he's an actor. He's kind of intense." She looked off and shrugged as if Griffin were no different from some guy she sat next to because their last names started with the same letter. She realized she was trying very hard to pretend Griffin was no one special.

"I'd watch out for him if I were you," Chris teased.

"Chris! We're just singing a song together."

"Hmm." Chris began to smile. "You must be a real professional. I wouldn't be able to keep my eyes off him if I were in your show."

Phoebe stood up triumphantly and clapped her hands. She was glad to have an excuse to shift the discussion to another topic. "Yay! Major progress has been made. You certainly can't accuse yourself of moping over Ted now!"

Chris actually started to giggle. That made Phoebe join in with her own bubbly, infectious laugh. She felt silly and a little giddy. It was nice to hear Chris laugh. It had been quite a while.

"Hey, Chris, look! Who's this?" Phoebe asked between gasps for air. She spread her eyes and pushed up her nose with her fingers. Chris called it her E.T. face and it never failed to crack her friend up.

"Ewww." Chris laughed. "Don't!"

Soon, they were both on a hopeless laughing jag. They'd even forgotten why they were giggling or what had started it, and neither one of them cared. It didn't matter. All that mattered was the physical act of laughing, that warm, friendly release.

When they finally calmed down, they gave each other a big hug and thought to themselves how lucky each were to have such a wonderful friend.

Once Phoebe got inside the theater, things turned serious. Instead of a rehearsal, where they spent time working on each separate number, Woody wanted to run quickly through each act so he could decide what order they should go in. That meant rushing through the rough spots or the parts kids hadn't learned. It also meant that for the first time, Phoebe could see all the other kids perform.

Blue Moon's rendition of "At the Hop" was lively and fun and Darrell Boldt got chuckles and applause with his inept juggling and right-on impersonation of Kennedy teachers. Phoebe could see Woody scratching his head — probably wondering if they could get away with some of Darrell's more biting jokes.

The actors were next. The first scene was be-

112

tween Griffin and Jerry Bates, a heavyset baseball player who could do a perfect deadpan expression. The contrast between Jerry's slow, un-
emotional style and Griffin's quick-tempered
charm made the sketch incredibly funny. Jerry
would sit there like a stone while Griffin sped
around the stage in an explosion of nervous
anxiety.

The sketch was one Woody had found. It was
a comedy routine from an English group called
Beyond the Fringe. The two boys played stran-
gers who had never met but insisted on acting as
if they knew each other. The more absurd it all
became, the funnier it was. Phoebe found herself
laughing as hard as she had with Chris before
rehearsal.

Griffin seemed to know just what to do to
make the audience laugh. Somehow, he understood what gesture or tone of voice they would
expect and then he would do just the opposite,
with hilarious results. Just a look, a turn of his
head would make them all bust up. Once Griffin
made them laugh by doing nothing, by literally
standing there like a statue. Phoebe was floored.

A monologue by Griffin came next. Everyone
was taken off guard when the piece began seriously with an explanation of all the terrible things
that had happened to this man, losing his job, his
wife, his self-respect.

At one point, he came down to the very edge
of the stage and sat down, his legs dangling below him. It was as if he were talking to each one
of them, as if each person were alone with him.
Phoebe saw real tears well up in Griffin's eyes

when he got to the part about his wife; she soon realized that her own cheeks were wet, too. At the very last moment, Griffin turned the whole thing into a joke with a line about how he was happy being unhappy. So the monologue ended on a funny and absurd note in keeping with the spirit of the Follies.

The thing that amazed Phoebe most was that Griffin was so at home on the stage. Instead of making him uncomfortable, the audience seemed to open him up like a huge flower. Phoebe couldn't help noticing how his face could change, at one moment handsome and boyish, then impish, then strong and single-minded. And his energy was extraordinary. He lit up the whole theater by himself.

When Griffin finished, the other kids clapped loud and long, some shaking their heads in appreciation. After a quick, humble bow, he climbed off the stage and sat in the back row. He wiped his face with a towel, slid down, and rested his legs on the seat in front of him.

"Great, great," said Woody, applauding. "You're all great! What can I say?" He looked down at his notebook. "There are still a few things to iron out, but considering that we have another week before the show, we're in great shape. Let's all take a break so Miss Weidemann can give me her brilliant advice, and then we'll run through the dancing acts."

Phoebe kept her eyes on Griffin, stretched out and looking up at the old ceiling as if he were searching for something he'd lost there. She wanted to go back and tell him how good he was, let him know how he had moved her. Slowly, she walked up the aisle and slipped into the seat next to him. She slid down to his level and waited for him to notice her.

When he turned to see who it was, he gave her a surprised but happy smile, as if she were just the person he wanted to see. Slunk low in their chairs, they felt somehow guarded, hidden from the others, like coconspirators.

Phoebe took a deep breath, intending to tell Griffin how wonderful she thought his acting was, and then he looked at her that way again. She couldn't speak. He moved his face closer to hers, slowly, never averting his eyes.

What's happening? Phoebe thought to herself. Suddenly, everything went into slow motion, as if the world had just changed dimension.

Oh my God, Phoebe thought, he's going to kiss me. Her heart was pumping so loudly that she wondered if he could hear it. Instead, his hand came up and brushed back a stray red curl that had straggled onto her forehead. Phoebe looked away.

"I was really impressed watching you act," she said at last in a shaky, almost desperate voice. She hadn't felt like this in a very long time, and it was starting to make her wonder just what it was she really felt for this boy. "You're very talented."

"Thanks. It was fun." Griffin's voice was a little weak, too. He cleared his throat and sat up. "I didn't know if people would laugh or not. Jerry did a great job. Playing the straight man isn't as easy as it looks."

"The two of you are such a funny pair," Phoebe rambled on. She wanted to keep talking. She *had* to keep talking. "I mean, you two are so different it reminds me of uh . . . uh . . . well . . ."

"Mutt and Jeff."

"No, not Mutt and . . ."

"Abbott and Costello."

"No," Phoebe stammered.

"How about Laurel and Hardy?"

"Well . . ."

"Cheech and Chong."

This made Phoebe laugh. Griffin's face crinkled up with humor, and he jokingly pushed Phoebe's shoulder. Suddenly, they were just two friends laughing — that was all, just two friends. It was as if that moment had never happened. Maybe it hadn't really taken place.

"Hey," Griffin said, "I do a two-part Cheech and Chong imitation, but I always need someone to do the other part."

"Well, I'm perfect," Phoebe joked.

"You know," Griffin affirmed, his eyes twinkling, "I bet you are."

Chapter
11

B*rad!! Where are you!!!* thought Phoebe as she looked for him after rehearsal. It was sort of stupid to try to find him because he had his Honda with him that day and she had her mom's station wagon. Even if she did find him, they couldn't ride home together. But that wasn't the point. All she knew was she wanted to see him, to see him right away. It had something to do with that scene with Griffin. Somehow, being with Brad might clear up her uncertainty.

Phoebe tried to remember what room Brad's committee meeting was in. He was listening to some group that wanted to start a smoking area on campus. That much she recalled from the notes she had typed up. She searched all the rooms surrounding the quad. They were all empty. Obviously, Brad had gone home.

The parking lot was almost deserted. Even over by the athletic field there were only a few cars. The sky had clouded up, and it was threatening to rain. Phoebe barely noticed. All she could think about was Griffin, and Brad, and how confusing it all was.

Every time her mind turned to Griffin, she got that breathless, warm feeling in the pit of her stomach. But what about Brad? Since she had begun going out with him, she had never felt this way about anyone else. Perhaps these feelings would pass and everything would return to normal. And yet, somehow, she sensed that "back to normal" was the last thing she wanted.

"Oh, Brad, why don't you show up?" Phoebe wailed out loud to the empty quad. But her boyfriend was nowhere around. She walked over to her mother's car, a subtle, nervous feeling in the pit of her stomach.

Half a mile away, Griffin Neill was walking swiftly home from school. It was a long way, almost three miles, but if he wanted to be in the show, he had to stay after the last school bus left. There was a city bus that stopped pretty close to his house, but it didn't come too often and Griffin was too impatient to wait for it.

Anyone who passed him could see that he was a young man who liked to move at a fast pace. Slim, long-legged, chin high, and back as straight as an arrow, Griffin enjoyed walking. En route, he could go over his lines and think about the rehearsal that day. His walks were the source of

118

some of his best ideas and inspirations for his acting.

He tried to walk a different route every day, exploring the main drags and the residential off-shoots. Today he was walking up Clear Spring Road, a narrow street lined with boxy brick houses and closely manicured lawns, when he was distracted by a sniffly whimper. Turning around to see what it was, he found a little girl, not more than four or five, standing on her lawn and staring up into a huge tree. She was starting to cry.

Griffin ran over to her and knelt down. "What's wrong?"

The little girl sniffed one or two more times, then wiped her cheek with her sleeve and pointed up into the tree. "Eliot, he can't get down."

Griffin looked up into the tree expecting to see an adventurous older brother, but Eliot turned out to be nothing more than a young kitten high up in the branches, about twenty feet off the ground. The kitten meowed when it saw Griffin.

Griffin patted the girl on the shoulder. "Don't worry, Eliot will be with you in a jiffy."

He put his book bag on the lawn and found a good place to plant his foot in the trunk of the tree. In no time at all, he was almost as high as Eliot. But every time he got close, Eliot seemed to want to climb a little higher.

"Eliot, don't do that'" the little girl shouted. "Let the man get you!"

Eliot didn't pay much attention as Griffin inched his way higher and the little girl held her breath. At this point, the front door of the house flew open and the little girl was joined by four brothers and sisters, two of whom appeared to be twins, and an elderly woman who looked like either a grandmother or a baby-sitter. The family craned their necks to get a good view of the rescue.

"Whoa," Griffin said, stretching his utmost to nab the kitten. "Eliot, you really know how to pick a view."

When Phoebe rounded the corner of Monument and Rose Hill Avenue, she made a U-turn and decided to drop over at Brad's. She hadn't seen his family in a couple of weeks, and she had an awful feeling that if she didn't stop and see him right now, she might never see him again. Ridiculous, she knew it was ridiculous, but that was the feeling she had.

When she turned onto Clear Spring Road, she couldn't help noticing the six people standing under a large, bare-limbed tree, looking up into it. Automatically, Phoebe slowed almost to a stop, stuck her head out the window, and looked up too.

For a moment, she felt very silly. After all, they were mostly kids standing around the tree. They were probably playing the game where you look up and see if you can make other people look up, too. Obviously she had just fallen for one of the oldest gags in the book. It wasn't until she ducked her head back into the car that she realized what they were looking at.

Without thinking, Phoebe turned off the engine and hopped out. By this time, Griffin was crawling up on the highest, thinnest branches of the old tree. The kitten was still scrambling out of reach. At last it seemed as though Griffin couldn't go any farther. But somehow, that's just what he did, and he managed to scoop up the kitten in one hand. There was a burst of applause. Griffin waved. Then, slowly, he began inching himself back down the tree. In less than a minute, he was back down with both feet on the ground.

"Thanks, Mister," the little girl cried as she took Eliot in her arms and began scolding him. "I promise he won't do it again."

Griffin chatted with the family until he noticed Phoebe standing only a few feet away. He stopped. Then he got an odd, almost embarrassed smile on his face and looked down at the ground. Phoebe backed up and leaned against her car. Finally, the family finished their thank-yous and retreated back into the house.

Griffin walked slowly over to Phoebe and leaned on the car alongside her.

"You'll do anything for applause, Neill," Phoebe said with a smile.

Griffin grinned. "Want to go back up there with me and do our duet?"

"I guess it couldn't be any scarier than the first time we sang together. I'd say we were out on a limb that day, too."

Griffin laughed and explained how he'd come across the cat and the little girl.

"You could have gotten hurt," Phoebe warned.

"No. Besides, who wants to go through life worrying about all the ways you might get hurt. My way of seeing it is if you want to do something, you ought to go as far as you can. I'd much rather break a few bones than miss things in life because I was afraid I might get hurt."

Phoebe was enjoying the conversation. At last, Griffin was sharing himself with her, off stage. And he seemed to be challenging her. She picked up the challenge eagerly.

"I'm not sure. I think you have to figure out what the dangers are so you can be prepared for them."

"Then you just get scared and freeze up. There's no surer way to fall on your face than to be thinking about the risk the whole time."

What a strange conversation, thought Phoebe. She and Brad certainly never talked about things like this. She held out her hand and felt a few droplets of rain.

"Do you live on this street?" she asked as she drew a face in the dust on her mother's car.

"I live on the other side of Frederick Avenue. You know, by the old railroad station, right behind Grovner's plant nursery."

Phoebe nodded. That was clear over on the other side of Rose Hill, almost in Leesberg. It had to be the very edge of the Kennedy school district.

"Is that your car?" Phoebe gestured towards a yellow Dodge parked across the street.

Griffin shook his head. "I like to walk," he answered proudly.

"You walk all the way to Grovner's? That's a long way! What do you do when it rains?"

"I get wet." Griffin bent down to pick up his book bag and slung it over his shoulder. "Think of all the things you miss when you ride in a car. Like today. I never would have seen that girl if I'd been speeding by. If I'd never seen her, I'd never have known what it was like to climb so far up in a tree. If I'd never climbed such a big tree I wouldn't have known how the ground looks from up there. You see?"

Phoebe wasn't sure. But she did know that she was fascinated.

"I want to experience everything there is to experience," continued Griffin, "meet every kind of person, feel every possible feeling."

Phoebe went with the conversation. It was somehow like Griffin's stare, intense and to the point. "But what about horrible, painful experiences. Why would you want to go through them?"

"See, that's what the great thing is about being an actor. Everything I do, whether it's good or bad, happy or sad, I can use it when I act. How could I act in a sad scene if I didn't know how it felt. Understand?"

Phoebe thought so. That's what made Griffin so compelling on stage. Everything he did there came from what he had seen or felt in real life. No wonder it was all so true when he acted.

Griffin went on, "I mean, I don't want to do anything where I'd have to hurt somebody else. But I have no reason to be afraid of whatever happens to me, because it will all be part of me and then it will also be part of Griffin the actor!" His voice rose with a proud ring. Just at that second, Griffin was answered by a far-off clap of thunder.

"Uh oh, we're going to get soaked," Phoebe said. "You may think that's a wonderful life experience, but it's one I've had a few times before. I've also experienced my mom yelling at me for coming home soaked." They both laughed. "Why don't I drive you home."

Griffin nodded, and they climbed into the front seat.

Just after they'd slammed the car doors shut, the rain began to fall in a soft, even sheet. They rolled up their windows and the windshield began to fog up. Being inside the car with Griffin made Phoebe suddenly self-conscious. He was so close to her. She felt light and happy, but confused, too, the way she had that afternoon, after Griffin had performed. Quickly she started the engine and pulled away from the curb.

"Do you know how to get to where I live?" Griffin asked.

"Sort of. My mom buys gardening stuff at Grovner's. I'll just need directions when we get to Frederick Avenue."

Griffin looked out the side window, and they drove in silence for a few minutes.

"Do you want to try to be an actor, I mean after high school?" Phoebe rubbed the inside of the windshield with an old handkerchief.

"I'm not going to *try* to be an actor, I am going to be an actor, period," Griffin came back at once.

There was no hostility in his voice, just determination. He leaned forward and cleaned his side of the windshield with the cuff of his sweat shirt.

"I don't mean to sound like I don't think you're good enough, 'cause I really think you are, I just meant . . ."

"I know. It's supposed to be such a hard profession. I don't care. That's what I want to do, and I'm going to go for it with everything I have. See, it's not like a regular job. Being an actor, well, it's going to be my life. And I don't care what I have to go through, I'm willing to risk it."

Phoebe stopped at a red light and looked at Griffin's expressive face. Hope and excitement were written all over it. He turned to her. "What about you, Phoebe?"

"What do you mean?"

"What about your singing? There's something really special about your voice. Do you know that?"

Phoebe blushed. "Well, I've always known I had a good voice. I was always picked first for choir, stuff like that. But being a professional singer, I don't think so."

"Why not?"

"Oh, maybe I'll give it a try later on. After I get my degree in computers or something like that. I guess you should have something to fall back on."

Griffin leaned forward and gestured passionately. "That's dumb! If you spend your time now learning something to fall back on, you'll never take a chance on doing what you really want to do. You have to take a chance, just dive in . . ."

"And hope you don't break your neck," Phoebe interrupted.

"That's one way of looking at it." Griffin smiled.

Griffin guided Phoebe across Frederick Avenue. She could see the greenery stocked in front of Grovner's nursery, so she knew they had to be close. Other than a few trips to buy plants, Phoebe had never been to this side of town. Slowing down, she realized that she didn't want the ride to be over so soon. She felt like she and Griffin had finally broken through some barrier that had stood between them, and she wanted to find out more and more about this interesting boy.

"Oh, wait," Phoebe said suddenly. "Isn't the Capitol Rink right near here?"

"You mean that ice skating rink? It's a little bit farther out on Frederick. Do you want to go ice skating?" Griffin sat up with a start. As soon as the idea occurred to him, he was anxious to follow it through.

"Do you like to skate?" Phoebe asked.

Griffin continued to speak excitedly. "I don't know, I've never tried it! But I bet it's fun. Let's go!"

Phoebe let loose with a lovely, free giggle. "Actually, what I was thinking about was going to visit a friend of mine. Do you know Lisa Chang? She goes to Kennedy."

"No, but I don't know a lot of kids at school."

"Well, neither does Lisa. She's at the rink much more often than she's at school. I bet she'll go to the Olympics to compete next time around. At least, she has a chance. We could drop over there and visit her. She's always asking me to come by." Phoebe paused. "Do you want to?"

"Sure," answered Griffin happily. There was no question or hesitation in his voice. "Let's go'"

Chapter
12

From the outside, the Capitol Ice Rink looked like an old supermarket — large, square, and slightly rundown. It was wedged between a used-car lot and a K-mart that had been there as long as Phoebe had lived in Rose Hill. There were only a few cars in the parking lot. The rain was beginning to let up, coming down light and soft.

"Something about this place remainds me of a circus tent," Phoebe commented as she climbed out of her car.

"It's that roof," agreed Griffin. They both stood for a moment in the drizzle and admired the huge corrugated metal roof before walking into the rink.

The double glass doors opened into a small foyer. An older man wearing a ski sweater appeared at a small window which was plastered with rink schedules and lesson notices. Phoebe could see into his office and counted three framed pictures of Lisa above his desk.

"Can I help you?" He had a thick European accent. "The public skating hours don't start again until seven o'clock tonight."

"We just wanted to visit our friend, Lisa Chang. Is that okay?" Phoebe asked while Griffin examined the trophy case on the opposite wall.

The man's face softened. "Ah, ya. She's through with her lesson, but she's still skating. You can go in and talk to her."

Phoebe could see a petite figure that looked like Lisa through the thick glass.

"Thanks." She turned to Griffin. "I'm going to call my mom and let her know where I am. Do you want to call home too?"

Griffin looked up with a surprised expression. "No," he answered simply, as if calling home were the farthest thing from his mind.

"Okay. Be back in a sec." Phoebe closed herself into the foyer phone booth and explained to her mom why she was running so late. She told her she was visiting Lisa but somehow forgot to mention Griffin.

The first thing Phoebe noticed about the inside of the rink was the sound. Tinny music over the loudspeaker competed with the shushing and scraping of skate blades. No shouting or laughing interrupted the intense concentration of the skaters. It made Phoebe feel like she wasn't supposed to talk, as though she were in a library.

The rink was a large oval of ice surrounded by hand rails and small bleachers on each of the long sides. Colorful flags from different nations waved over the corners. It was a world all its own, from the damp wood smell to the cold of the air to the unspoken rules that governed the etiquette on the ice.

Phoebe and Griffin sat on the bench closest to the rink and were instantly mesmerized. Obviously, this was an hour reserved for advanced skaters only, and the fifteen or so who filled the rink were all graceful and sure of themselves. No one, however, compared with Lisa. She was in the center of the rink, her face tense with concentration as she lifted her arms over her head, arched her back, and flew into a spin with one leg bent and raised behind her. As she spun, her shoulder-length black hair whipped around. In her lavender skating skirt, white sweater and tights, and pink wool gloves, she looked like one of those beautiful miniatures that twirl atop a child's music box.

It seemed as if every other skater knew Lisa was special and gave her constant right-of-way, space, and respect. Two younger girls leaned on the opposite railing, never taking their eyes off her. She worked on the same spin a few more times until she joined the flow around the rink and started to practice jumping. With an effortless approach, she would take off from the ice, spin around faster than seemed humanly possible and land just as easily. Each time, Griffin and Phoebe gasped.

Phoebe was beginning to feel the cold, and she didn't move away when Griffin slid closer. His arm rested against hers as they both hunched forward to watch the skaters. Phoebe couldn't help noticing she was shaking a bit. She wasn't sure if that was caused by the cold or by Griffin's touch.

At last, Lisa whooshed to a stop and spotted her old friend.

"Phoebe!" she cried happily. "Hi!" The girls shared a hug over the railing. Lisa looked around. "Is Brad here too?" she asked brightly.

Phoebe felt her throat tighten. She knew that Griffin was looking at her, but she couldn't return his gaze. "No, uh, he had a meeting after school. You know, for student government." She cleared her throat, then added nervously, "He says hi, though."

"Tell him hi, too. I haven't seen him in ages." Lisa looked at Griffin with curiosity.

"This is my friend, Griffin Neill. We're in the Follies at school together." Griffin nodded hello.

"Hi. It's great that you came by. Let's go in the snack bar. They have pretty good hot chocolate." Lisa hopped up on the rubber matting, grabbed a pair of plastic skate guards from off of the bench, and slipped them over her skate blades. The three of them walked into the tiny snack bar and got big cups of hot cocoa, then sat down at a small round table.

"You are incredible," Griffin said to Lisa as he blew on his cocoa.

Lisa smiled shyly. "Thanks. I have a long way to go, though. I may look good compared to the people here, but you should see the real competition winners. They make me look like a total klutz."

"I can't believe that," Phoebe chimed in.

131

"Really, it's so amazing to watch you. Is it as much fun as it looks?"

Lisa laughed. "Sometimes. Like today, when I'm done working with my coach and I can just practice on my own, that's really fun. But being in competition and waiting for the judges to hold up those score numbers is not so much fun, believe me."

"But it must be outrageous to skate when this rink is full of people and they're all watching you. Wow, hearing them all gasp at the same time, that must be such a high." Griffin's face was full of wonder.

"Not always," Lisa said wistfully. "I remember this one time in a competition when I went out to the middle of the ice to start my program. Instead of cheering, the whole crowd was booing. It was so awful. They were booing because they didn't like the scores that the judges had given the skater before me. It really freaked me out. I almost started crying right there on the ice. I knew the crowd wasn't booing me, but my nerves were really frazzled by it. Sometimes I like having an audience, but sometimes I wish I could just skate because I like to skate, not for other people."

Griffin listened intently.

"Like now. I'm working on a triple toe loop. That may not mean much to you, but up until now, I've been doing a double toe loop. That means I've been turning around twice on this one jump, and now I'm turning around three times."

Phoebe and Griffin nodded.

"Anyway, the first few times I actually did it

in practice, I just about went nuts I was so excited. It was sort of like flying, like being weightless or like being a bird or something." Lisa looked embarrassed. "Plus, it's kind of a big deal to be able to do one because not that many skaters can."

"That's great," Griffin cut in with an amazed tone in his voice.

Lisa smiled. "Well. The thing is, when I work on it alone, it's really fun; but doing it in a competition, then I'll be so nervous that I'll just be praying I don't fall."

"And I bet that's a sure way to fall," remarked Griffin with a look to Phoebe.

"That's right," answered Lisa. "So that's why I sometimes wish I could just skate for myself."

Griffin drew in an excited breath. "Would you do it for us? Your triple loop jump, or what did you call it?"

"Triple toe loop." Lisa shrugged happily and downed the rest of her cocoa. "Okay. Just remember, I'm still working on it."

Phoebe and Griffin held on to their cups and followed Lisa back to the rink. She slipped off her skate guards and glided onto the ice. Phoebe and Griffin leaned against the rail.

Lisa began stroking around the rink, each slide graceful and strong. Once, twice, Lisa completed her triple toe loop, and even though her landing was unsteady, the jump was breathtaking. It was as though she had broken through the boundaries of human movement and had the speed that Phoebe and Griffin had experienced only in dreams.

Griffin was completely absorbed in watching this exquisite girl. When Phoebe looked at his face, she was surprised to feel something that she hadn't felt for a long time. Her jaw became tense and her hands clasped the railing a little too tightly. Phoebe knew very well what the feeling was. Jealousy. She was actually jealous that Griffin was so taken with Lisa! With a slightly hurt expression on her face, Phoebe took a deliberate step away from Griffin. Folding her bare arms around herself, her teeth began to chatter from the damp cold.

Then, without warning, she felt Griffin step next to her. His sweat-shirted arm wrapped around her shoulder.

"Cold?" he whispered, looking into her eyes that way again.

"A little," was all she could answer.

Just then, they saw a blur of lavender and white as Lisa went into another spinning jump. But just as she was about to land, her balance went off and she fell on the ice with an ungraceful whack. Sitting on her bottom in a very awkward position, Lisa expressed a quick second of shock before getting right back up and out of the way of the other skaters. Phoebe and Griffin were getting ready to run onto the ice in their street shoes, but Lisa was already skating over to the railing with a silly smile on her beautiful face. She brushed beads of water off of her tights and gloves.

"Are you okay?" Phoebe asked urgently.

"Oh, yeah." Lisa giggled. "It looks like it hurts a lot more than it really does. It's not like falling on the floor or anything. That's because the ice is softer than the ground and you slide, so you almost never get hurt. I think I've fallen as many times as I've been up on skates!"

Griffin squeezed Phoebe's arm meaningfully.

"Let's just hope I don't do that in my next competition. I could call it the special Lisa Chang triple toe splat!"

Phoebe still looked concerned.

"Don't worry. I've seen tons of skaters fall in the Olympics, you just get right back up and hope you didn't look like too much of a klutz when you were down." Lisa's giggle was infectious. They all began to laugh.

"Are you sure you're not hurt?" cautioned Phoebe.

"Sure. Watch." Lisa skated towards the corner of the rink and took off in another spirited triple toe loop. This time, her landing was perfect. As she came out of it another skater gave her a big smile and a thumbs up. Lisa's face was radiant. "All right! That's the first time I haven't gunked up the finish!"

"See, Phoebe, it's just like I was telling you. If you never let yourself fall you never get any better," Griffin whispered. Phoebe turned full face to look at him. His blue-gray eyes were focused and intent, his shoulders thrust back proudly. She came just up to the bottom of his chin, and for a second she longed to lean her face forward into the crook of his neck and just rest there, sharing his warmth and strength. She didn't move.

"My dad's going to pick me up pretty soon," said Lisa after skating one more time around the rink. "Do you guys need a ride home?"

"No, thanks." Phoebe quickly looked at her watch. "I have my mom's car. I gotta go, too. It's getting late."

"When are the Follies?" Lisa peeled off her wet gloves.

"Next Friday night. Can you come?" Griffin asked.

"I'll try. I have practice until six and jazz class at seven. Maybe I can come to the second half."

"Well, you should try because Phoebe's singing is pretty special."

Griffin gave Phoebe a warm smile that couldn't have gone unnoticed by Lisa. Phoebe was glad that her friend was not a gossip.

"I'll try. I remember hearing you sing in some seventh-grade assembly, but not since then," Lisa said with a smile.

"Well, I hope I sing a little better than I did in seventh grade. Anyway, if you can come, that would be great, if not, I understand."

Lisa leaned over the rail to give Phoebe a good-bye hug. Suddenly her dark eyes looked a little sad. "Come and visit me again, both of you. I never talk to anybody anymore, that is except for other skaters and my coach and stuff. I miss my old friends."

"Okay," Phoebe assured her. "I'll probably see you at school anyway."

Griffin and Lisa said good-bye, and he walked on ahead. Phoebe started to follow, when Lisa skated to the far corner and motioned Phoebe over. Griffin gave Phoebe a nod as if he understood that Lisa wanted to talk to her alone.

"Are things okay with you and Brad?" Lisa asked in a low voice. Phoebe looked back over at Griffin, who was reading notices on the wall near the entrance. "Did you two break up or something?"

Phoebe wasn't sure what to say. "No, we didn't break up. We're still together."

Lisa looked in Griffin's direction. "Oh." There was an awkward silence. Lisa broke it with a sunny smile. "Well, I promise I'll try to come and see the Follies." She pushed off and gave a cheery wave.

Phoebe waved back and watched Lisa's tiny, strong figure blend in with the other skaters. She quickly joined Griffin, and they walked out to the car.

The rain had stopped, but a layer of dark clouds hung over the sky, making it look later than it really was. Without speaking, Griffin and Phoebe climbed into the station wagon, and Phoebe started the engine. She was glad Griffin realized Lisa had wanted to talk to her about something private and that he tactfully didn't ask any questions. "Which way to your house?" Phoebe asked, as she pulled out of the parking lot.

Griffin paused and leaned back against the seat. "Turn left at the nursery."

Phoebe drove past Grovner's and onto a small street that she had never been on before. One side was lined with little wooden houses and the other with two- and three-story brick apartments.

The lawns were overgrown and littered with toys, and most of the houses were in need of repainting.

"It's the building on the left." Griffin pointed to a plain brick apartment house with a row of ragged bushes in front. The old building was shaped like a U, with a scruffy lawn in the middle. The lawn was the playground for two screeching seven-year-olds and a diapered toddler. An overweight woman sat on the steps smoking a cigarette.

"This is where you live?" Phoebe asked.

She hadn't meant to sound so surprised, but it had slipped out nonetheless. It was just that the rundown apartment house was so different from the neat, roomy homes of the rest of her friends. Phoebe parked, but Griffin made no immediate move to get out of the car.

"Will your mom get mad at you for being so late?" she asked, wondering if her mother was testily waiting dinner for her.

"Why should she?" Griffin asked simply.

"Well, I don't know," said Phoebe. "Maybe because she made dinner and it's getting cold or because you're supposed to be home at a certain time and that's just the way it is."

"My mom trusts me. I'm free to do what I want." Griffin faced her.

"Really?"

"Sure. Mom has worked full-time since my folks split up, so I just come and go as I please. She knows I can take care of myself."

"My mom works too, but . . . well, it's not that she doesn't trust me, but . . . you know, there are

138

a lot of rules. Nothing unfair, maybe she's a little strict sometimes, but not bad." Phoebe leaned over the steering wheel. "When did your folks split up?"

Griffin looked out the window. "When I was little. I barely even remember my dad. I never see him."

"Oh," sighed Phoebe sympathetically.

"Hey, it's okay." Griffin smiled. "I love having so much freedom. If I want to stay up all night and go over my lines, I can do it. I'm totally my own person."

Phoebe's mouth fell open. "Your mom lets you stay up all night!"

"Well not if she's home, but she stays in D.C. with her boyfriend a lot of the time so I really have a great situation. You can't find out very much about life if you have to be home every day at five o'clock." Griffin picked his book bag up off of the car floor.

"What about grades and homework. Doesn't your mom bug you about that stuff?"

Griffin pushed up the sleeves of his sweat shirt and leaned on his forearms. "That's up to me. It's like this. The classes I like, the ones I think are interesting and meaningful, I do great in those. The ones that are just a waste, I don't bother with. I think that's the best way to do it. I can spend a lot of time getting really good at what's important and not worry about learning all the stuff I'll never use again."

Phoebe thought about the headaches she got studying for computer math. "Don't you want to go to college?"

"I just want to be a great actor and have interesting experiences. I don't know if college is going to help me with that or not."

Phoebe took a deep breath and let her head fall back. Everything about Griffin was rare and unusual. She couldn't imagine any kid in her crowd saying he or she didn't care about college. Part of Phoebe was shocked that Griffin was so easygoing about his future, but mostly she was filled with interest and respect. What Griffin was doing took real guts. It was safe to be pre-med like Brad, even though, of course, it was hard and a lot of work. But Brad would be in school forever and not really have to worry about anything other than studying and passing tests. Griffin, on the other hand, was diving into life face first, willing to taste and experience everything. He had real courage.

Griffin started to reach for the door handle but turned back to Phoebe instead. "Phoebe."

"Hmm." She saw that look in his eyes again. His face looked boyish and expectant. He leaned in toward her. "I guess I want to say" — he paused and cleared his throat — "that I don't want the Follies to be over."

The air was very still, as if every word carried enormous weight. Phoebe was both scared and hopeful at the same time.

"I know what you mean," Phoebe finally admitted.

Griffin smiled sadly. "Maybe we'll still get to see each other. Who knows what could happen."

With that, he swept out of the car and left Phoebe to deal with what he had just said. She watched him pat one of the kids on the head and run up the stairs, taking two steps in each leap. Before he disappeared into the building, he turned and gave an energetic wave.

Phoebe leaned her head on the steering wheel to calm herself before starting the car. Then, she flicked the radio on full volume and began to sing. By the time she got home, her voice was drowning out the radio, and she couldn't have cared less who in Rose Hill heard.

Chapter
13

It was Monday morning and Laurie had had a long weekend. There had been the usual distractions, the pool, her stereo, MTV on her father's giant video screen, and talking on her phone, but none of them had been quite enough to get her mind off Peter Lacey. She had to have him, it was as simple as that. But Laurie knew it wasn't going to be easy.

Peter was not only handsome (incredibly so), cool, witty, and very much his own person, he was also notoriously immune to love. People said the only thing he really loved was WKND, and no girl would ever replace the radio station. Well, maybe that was true.

They always said the same kind of thing about Captain Kirk and the *Enterprise* on old *Star Trek* reruns. Captain Kirk could never love a woman because he loved only his ship. But there was one big difference between Peter and Captain Kirk

— Captain Kirk was a television character, Peter Lacey was a real live guy.

Still, it wasn't going to be easy. So far, there was little sign that he had fallen for her. She would just have to work a little harder. Actually, the challenge made him all the more desirable.

The key, she decided, was going to be her party. Between her father, her father's stereo and video equipment, and Laurie's new dress, Peter didn't have a chance.

By lunchtime, Laurie felt confident. Today, she was going in for her second and final lesson from Peter on how to broadcast over the radio station. She had to make sure she looked good, so first, she went to the girls' bathroom. It was crowded, but Laurie squeezed into the best space, right in front of the mirror. Her short dark hair looked just right, brushed back on one side and forward over one eye on the other. It was one of her hair stylist Ursula's better cuts. Laurie tied a lightweight scarf around her head the way she'd seen in *Vogue*. It worked. With an extra dab of the perfume her father had brought her from Paris, Laurie was ready for the radio station.

Laurie marched down the long corridor to the broadcasting booth, her shapely legs smacking against the hem of her short, straight skirt. She slid out of her wide-shouldered leather jacket and let it hang over her back by one finger. Then, she walked into the studio.

Where was Peter's assistant, Janie Barstow? Usually Janie was standing guard in the hall to make sure no one distracted Peter or made too

143

much noise. Because the funky studio was so airless, Peter often left the door open, even when he was on the air, so Janie had to patrol the area. But today, the hallway was empty.

A shy laugh rolled out of the booth, and Laurie looked through the window to find Janie and Peter inside. They were sharing a sandwich and giggling over something in a magazine. Laurie shook her head. Janie Barstrow was truly one of the plainest girls she had ever seen and one of the all-time worst dressers. Too tall, too thin, too mousy, and too blah, that was what Laurie thought of Janie. She didn't know how Peter could even stand to work with her.

"Yoo hoo," said Laurie, leaning in the doorway to the booth. Peter and Janie looked up. They both had their mouths full, and Peter was holding a copy of *National Lampoon*.

Janie immediately jumped up and almost bowed to Laurie.

"Hi, Laurie," she said nervously as she got up to leave. She stopped and turned back to Peter. "Do you need anything, Peter?" she asked.

"Let's see." Peter looked around while he downed a carton of chocolate milk. "Toss me the Police single and the new Cars album. Thanks for the sandwich." He smiled.

Janie backed away into the hall.

"Hey, Laur, what's up?" Peter said easily. He leaned back in his chair and rested his feet on the control board, then causually batted a ball of tinfoil at the window in front of him.

Laurie tossed her jacket over the control panel

and hiked herself up against it. "Hey, there," she said with a smile.

"Hey, could you not put your jacket on there? I have a record which is going to be up in a few seconds."

Laurie good-naturedly removed her jacket. She continued to lean against the board.

"So what's going on? The party's this weekend, isn't it?"

Laurie nodded. "Saturday at eight. You'll be there, right? I'm counting on you to do the music."

"Oh, sure. Why not?" Peter shrugged. He pushed a hunk of brown hair out of his eyes and started snapping his fingers to a rhythm in his head. "So, did you need to tell me something?"

Laurie resisted an impulse to scream. She knew Peter was possessive of his radio station, but he should have remembered that she was coming for her lesson today. After all, she'd be starting to do the activities update spots the following week. She reminded him.

"Oh, right! Man, I keep forgetting about that for some reason. As of next week, we'll be partners, so to speak." Peter drummed on his stomach and looked up at the white ceiling.

"So to speak," repeated Laurie in her sexiest voice.

Peter stopped drumming. "Yeah, well, let's go over all this stuff again."

He reviewed what he had showed her before, stopping every few minutes to introduce records and continue the on-air patter for which he was famous.

145

The first time he went on the air, Laurie shut the door. She did not reopen it. Actually, she was taking advantage of the teeny space to work on Peter. Every time he showed her a button or a dial, she leaned in to examine it. When she asked a question, she managed to touch his hand for emphasis. She noticed that Peter was getting nervous and smiled to herself — it was all working.

"One last thing, Laur," Peter said jumpily. "Uh, just remember not to cough or clear your throat or anything right into the microphone. It sounds really dorky." He let out a short, choppy laugh.

Laurie smiled and moved up very close to him. Her face was no more than two or three inches from his. She looked at him with her big brown eyes and let loose with an innocent smile. "Don't worry. I promise to do everything just right." Her voice was low and breathy.

"Yeah, I know, but it's, like, easy to forget that kind of thing when . . ."

Peter was beginning to feel self-conscious. He could feel the dampness against the back of his neck and under his fifties bowling shirt. The room was small and close, but Laurie was even closer. Peter usually didn't even notice the many girls who had crushes on him, and so they finally would just give up. But Laurie was too obvious not to notice. Besides, it wasn't like she was all giggly and nervous and afraid to talk to him. In fact, she was making *him* feel silly and nervous. Peter had never had a girl so obviously seductive with him. Especially a girl who looked like Laurie Bennington.

Laurie ran a hand slowly through her thick hair. Cocking her head to one side, she finished the motion by resting the hand on Peter's shoulder.

"Peter," she began, "make sure to tell your folks that you're going to be out very late Saturday night when you come to my party." She smiled as if they had shared a private joke. "I told my father all about you, and he really wants to meet you. He thinks he might even have a summer job for you at one of his cable TV stations."

"Honest!" Peter couldn't help saying.

"Honest," Laurie repeated in a rosy voice. "But he's coming in from London the day of the party and he might not get to the house until late." Actually, that wasn't exactly true. Her father was coming in the night before the party, but she stretched the truth just a tiny bit. She began to trace Peter's features with her manicured fingertip. "So, if you want to meet him, you may have to stay late after everybody else leaves. You wouldn't mind that too much, would you?"

Peter shook his head. He felt like a puppet and Laurie was pulling the strings.

"I'm sure you and I can find something to do while we wait for him." Laurie smiled. She closed her eyes and started to kiss him. Peter felt like he was holding on to the edge of a cliff with only one hand. All he needed was the slightest nudge, and he'd go over. His eyes started to close as Laurie's face lifted to his.

147

"Peter!!!" screeched a shrill, upset voice. Peter open his eyes to see a very distressed Janie Barstow standing in the doorway. It was hard to tell who was more embarrassed, Peter or Janie. Discovery didn't seem to bother Laurie at all.

Janie's long face was as red as a lobster. She looked like she was about to cry. "Peter, you're on! I mean, The Police are finished! The song is over and nothing's going out over the radio!"

Peter looked at Janie for one tiny moment of disbelief and then spun around to the first turntable. As quickly as possible, he threw an album on and turned the volume dials without bothering to introduce it. He couldn't believe he had let himself be so distracted that he had messed up his radio show.

Laurie simply gave Janie a dirty look and backed into the corner. She leaned back on one leg, her high-heeled foot resting against the wall.

Peter was frantic. After Janie stormed back into the hallway, her face a mixture of shock and anger, he sat in his chair and leaned forward with his head in his hands.

"Geez, I can't believe I did that," he cried. "I've been doing this show for almost a year, and I've never let myself space out and let the air go dead like that! Man, that's terrible!"

He banged his fist against the control board. Laurie stayed in the corner and waited for him to calm down. Peter turned on the studio speakers and let the music blast into the booth. He waited for the song to finish and then went back on the air.

148

"Hey, Cardinals, sorry about that little moment of ozone there. Even Peter Lacey has his funky days. Hope to make it up to you with the last disc of the day. It's the latest from The Talking Heads, and I hope you like it. This is Peter Lacey of WKND signing off until tomorrow." Peter brought up the volume on the record and switched off his mike. He let out a heavy sigh and shook his head angrily.

"Peter," Laurie said softly.

"Yeah. What?" His voice was edgy and tense.

"I'm really sorry." Laurie looked down, trying to seem terribly upset.

"Huh?" Peter was surprised to hear Laurie apologize.

"I'm sorry I, uh, distracted you while you were working. That was really thoughtless of me."

Peter looked up. "It wasn't your fault, Laurie. It was totally my fault."

Laurie's voice began to sound teary. "It's just that I really like you," she said daintily. She hoped she looked as though she were about to cry. "I guess I just got carried away. Please don't be mad at me."

"I'm not mad, Laur."

"Are you sure?" Laurie came over and knelt by his chair. She looked up at him with the most innocent eyes. "I couldn't stand it if you were mad at me. I couldn't stand it if you didn't come to my party. You see, I have this feeling that there's something really strong between you and me and I'm just giving in to it. Don't you feel it too?"

"Uh . . ."

149

"It's okay. Just promise me you won't be mad about today."

"I promise. I already told you I wasn't mad."

"Thank you. You are a very special person, Peter. I can't wait for my father to meet you. I'm sure he'll be incredibly impressed." Laurie stood up slowly and slung her jacket over her shoulder. "Remember to tell your folks you'll be out late on Saturday, okay?"

"Okay," Peter repeated.

Laurie leaned forward and kissed Peter on the lips. The kiss was very quick and light. Peter's eyes were opened wide with shock.

"Bye," whispered Laurie as she left. When she passed Janie sitting at a little desk, Janie wouldn't even look up. Laurie smiled to herself. "Bye, Janie. See you later!" she called back.

Laurie was positively aglow as she walked back into the quad. Everything was set. She had asked her father to stay out late the night of her party, so that it would be at least two o'clock before he came home. That would give her a couple of hours alone with Peter. By the time her father finally made his appearance, Peter Lacey would be her steady boyfriend.

When Phoebe saw Laurie bounding across the quad at the end of lunch period, she remembered about the party. She hated to admit it, but she was glad Brad wouldn't be getting there until late. Somehow, it felt weird to be with him now.

When they were together, Phoebe felt and acted distant. And she wasn't sure what to do about it. This weekend, she had avoided their

Saturday night date by telling him she had a stomach ache. He had been sympathetic, had even dropped by to bring her some special herb tea that Sasha had recommended. That kind of thing made it even harder. Just when Phoebe allowed herself to consider the possibility she and Brad might not always be together, he would go and do something like bringing her special herb tea.

"How's your tum, Pheeb?" Brad asked as they walked to fifth period. All during lunch, some dumb freshman had been asking him about how to run for student government. Brad couldn't get rid of the nerdy kid, and Phoebe hadn't been able to get a word in edgewise.

"It's a lot better. The tea helped a whole bunch." Phoebe smiled sadly. Brad looked very handsome today. He was wearing his letterman's sweater with his swimming letter from the previous year. He put his arm around her shoulder softly.

"I missed you," he said sweetly. "I guess I'm so used to seeing you all the time I don't even think about it. But this weekend, when we didn't go out, I guess I got to thinking about stuff, you know, you and me and how things have been the last week or so. I, uh, felt kinda bad."

Phoebe turned to face him. His brown eyes were full of concern, and she could tell how hard it was for him to say this. They were in the crowded first floor hall, so it was impossible to continue an intimate conversation against the hollering of other kids and slamming of locker doors. Phoebe took Brad's hand and led him to a small, quiet corner outside the chemistry lab. He followed willingly.

"Pretty noisy, huh?" Phoebe laughed nervously.

"Word War Three," joked Brad. Suddenly, he moved close and took Phoebe in his arms. He hugged her so tightly, it was as if he were trying to squeeze out all the bad feelings that had come between them. Phoebe breathed in his familiar soapy smell and closed her eyes. The warmth of his broad chest was so safe and familiar. She put her arms around his neck and hugged him back. At last, they separated and looked into each other's eyes.

"Pheeb, I'm sorry if I take you for granted sometimes. I know I get really involved in my own thing, and I guess sometimes maybe I forget about you. If being in the Follies is such a big deal for you, then it's good that you're in them." He touched her chin. "I mean it."

"It *is* a big deal for me," Phoebe admitted. She stood up very straight.

"I guess I get so wrapped up in everything, student government and college and all, that it's easy for me to forget you have things which are important to you, too. What I mean to say is, I'm still sorry you can't go to Princeton with me, but I'm also sorry I can't see you in the Follies."

Phoebe smiled broadly. She never thought she'd hear Brad say anything like this, and could tell from the look in his eyes that he meant every word.

"So," Brad continued, "I just hope when this

is all over and you're a huge hit in the show and I wow all those big guns at Princeton, the two of us get back to normal. What do you think?"

The bell rang for the beginning of fifth period. There were only four minutes before the tardy bell, and Phoebe had to get all the way up to the third floor for French.

"I think that's a good idea." Phoebe smiled.

She felt more for Brad in this moment than she had in the last month. Standing on her tiptoes, she gave him a kiss. He walked her back into the hall and waved to her as she raced up the stairs. When Phoebe reached the second floor, she looked down between the staircases and saw Brad still standing there watching her.

Chapter
14

Brenda Austin was confused.

Her large brown eyes didn't seem confused. Her long, dark hair, smooth skin, and high cheekbones were as beautiful as always. In fact, most other girls at Kennedy took one look at Brenda and were envious. They could see instantly that she was a girl of uncommon, almost bewitching, beauty. Brenda was sixteen, but she could sometimes pass for eighteen or more. Older college guys asked her on dates. In the past she'd actually been able to get into clubs and bars.

All of this should have made Brenda feel fortunate, even privileged, but she didn't. Not with the kinds of expectations her family had of her. Sometimes, she thought they wished they could trade her in for a new model, like a car. Take Chris, for instance. Her stepsister wished Brenda were the kind of person to fit in with the

154

popular crowd, but when she tried, all she got was a humiliating snub from Laurie Bennington. Her mother wanted her to make an effort to get along with Chris, but when she made an attempt things between the sisters got even worse. Her stepfather wanted her to do better in school, yet even when her grades went up, he never seemed to be satisfied. All he seemed to talk about were the opportunities Brenda had already missed by not having attended this school or that school, by not taking Latin or French, other stuff like that. And nobody wanted her to see her friends at the halfway house, and *they* were the only ones who really liked and understood her.

Trying to figure it all out, Brenda walked toward downtown Rose Hill after school. There was a bookstore in the tiny Mill Creek shopping center where she loved to browse. It was called The Albratross. She liked the absurdity of a bookstore named after such a strange bird. What she also liked about the bookstore was that you could wander around, even sit on the floor and read for as long as you wanted, and no one would bother you. The owners didn't seem to care if you bought anything or not.

The Albatross was owned by Mr. and Mrs. Jenkins, a couple who were as old as her parents but dressed like college students in faded jeans and colorful old T-shirts. The Jenkins were both soft-spoken, kind, and in love with books. Brenda knew their daughter Sasha. She was in Chris's crowd and wrote for the school newspaper. She was one of the few people in the group who Brenda thought was really nice. Once Brenda had seen Sasha in the store, and Sasha had actually smiled warmly. The Albatross was the one place in Rose Hill where Brenda felt at home.

Often, when Brenda's parents accused her of having gone to the halfway house after school to hang out with her friends, she had really been at the bookstore. But she never defended herself or told her parents where she really went. Maybe, deep down, she wanted them to keep misunderstanding her. That was what Tony Martinez, the counselor at the halfway house, had told her. He had suggested that maybe Brenda secretly wanted to remain the bad sister. She wondered if that were true. A negative identity was better than no identity at all.

Of course, sometimes Brenda did take the bus into Georgetown to visit the halfway house. A lot of the kids who had once been there came back to visit. She liked talking with Tony, because he was so supportive and wise. She also liked being in a place where she didn't stick out as different. At the halfway house, she could be totally herself.

But after school on Monday, Brenda wanted to go to the bookstore. As she walked in, she noticed with relief that The Albatross was as relaxed and busy as ever. She took off her sunglasses and hung them on the neck of her sweater. This wasn't a place where you needed to hide your eyes. Like at the halfway house, she could really be herself here.

Brenda wandered slowly over to the last aisle.

It was crowded with dusty shelves and racks, and the side wall was plastered with notices. Her favorite section was the one with the psychology books. It didn't matter if the books were trendy paperbacks with photos of sunburned authors on the back or large, official-looking textbooks. She found them all interesting. She picked out one that immediately caught her eye.

In the back corner of the bookstore were a round wooden table and three straight-backed chairs. Mr. Jenkins was sitting in one, and he was writing in a clothbound notebook. When Brenda sat in the chair next to him, he smiled and scratched his graying beard.

Brenda had pulled down a book called *Assertiveness for Women*. The gist of it was that lots of women and girls felt the need for a lot of reassurance from the people around them, and so they never got mad and talked about what they really felt or wanted. Brenda ran her hand through her fine, layered hair. That certainly wasn't true of her. She had no trouble getting mad. Although, as she read further, she began to recognize in herself some of the defensive patterns the book described. The defense she used was called "passive resistance." The book explained passive resistance as not getting outwardly angry when something bothered you, but keeping it inside and letting it simmer. The book said it was better to tell other people how you felt than to mope and withdraw.

Brenda thought about the incident with Laurie Bennington and the football game. In a way, Brenda had been very assertive with Laurie. She had told her off. And yet, reading this book, she wondered if lashing out and then running away wasn't a perfect example of not really dealing with anger?

Perhaps all she had done was prove to Laurie and Chris that she really was a creep. It might have been better if she'd been able to stay calm and explain to Laurie that she had treated her cruelly. Of course, it was always easy to think of the right thing to say after the fact. Maybe if she ever got another chance, she might be able to explain to Laurie with calmness and dignity that, yes, Brenda Austin was a person with feelings, too!

It was getting late, so Brenda put the book back on the shelf and started to leave the store. Mrs. Jenkins, who recognized her as a regular visitor, waved good-bye as the dark-haired girl walked out into the small parking lot. Before going home, Brenda decided to call the halfway house and talk to a few of her friends. It was too awkward to call from home, so Brenda liked to use the phone booth outside the Rexall drugstore.

"Garfield House," answered an official-sounding young voice.

"Hi, this is Brenda Austin. I'm just calling to see who's hanging out there. You know, just to say hi," Brenda chatted.

"Brenda, this is Danny. How ya doin!"

Brenda smiled. Danny was a sixteen-year-old boy who had been staying at Garfield House when she had spent her week there. Danny didn't have it easy. His mother was an alcoholic, and he had moved to the halfway house when his mom had gone away to some special clinic for treatment. He was a sweet, stocky kid who often wore a sleeveless denim vest with his name embroidered across the back. He was a favorite friend of Brenda's.

"What are you doing answering the phone?"

"Hey, I'm working here now, helpin' out. I answer the phone, help Tony organize the rap sessions, stuff like that."

A lot of kids who had been through Garfield House came back later to work. They considered it an honor to help Tony with his famous daily therapy sessions.

"That's great! How's your mom doing?"

"Pretty good. She doesn't like her new job too much, but she's still not drinking, and so that's all right." Danny's voice was bright, with a little bit of toughness. "How about you? How's doings at home?"

"Oh, it's still kind of hard, but I *am* doing better in school. I don't think I'm going to win the Miss Congeniality award. My social life is pretty depressing," Brenda said, trying to laugh off her words.

"Well, hey, what do you say we go out and do something Saturday night? It would be great to see you."

"Okay!" agreed Brenda instantly. "What do you want to do?"

"Hold on. There's a kid who just got here today and he has a car. How about if he comes, too? His name is Ray, and he seems like an all-right guy." Danny covered the phone and yelled to Ray, asking if he wanted to join them and

159

provide transportation. Ray yelled back yes in a deep, boisterous voice. "Did you hear that?" Danny asked.

"Sure did," Brenda answered.

"Hey, maybe we can go see the new *Conan the Barbarian* movie. It's playing here in Georgetown."

Brenda wrinkled up her nose. Boys always liked dumb movies like that. Suddenly, a different idea occurred to her. Her brain started whirling as if a spark of electricity had just hit her. Of course! Why hadn't she thought of it before? She knew exactly what she wanted to do this Saturday night.

"Danny, I have a better idea." She paused and took a deep breath. "I know of this huge, fancy party that a friend of my sister's is throwing. Maybe you and I and Ray should drop by and see if it's any good."

Brenda chuckled to herself. Ever since she had overheard Laurie on the telephone, she had kept the information about the party in the back of her mind. It would be interesting to see how Laurie reacted to having the three of them show up. It would also be a great time for her to tell Laurie why she'd gotten so upset the day of the Leesberg football game. She'd be calm and eloquent as she explained everything, just the way that psychology book had suggested. "Yeah, I think we really should check out this party," Brenda stressed.

"You mean like crash it?" Danny sounded uneasy.

"It's okay. My sister and her whole crowd

160

will be there. I don't want to stay long, anyway. I just want to make an appearance. That's the important thing." And it really was important, Brenda told herself. She didn't want to be left out once again. She needed to feel like she was part of things at Kennedy.

"All right. I guess that'll be good. I'll pick you up at eight or so?"

"I'll be in the parking lot of the Mill Creek shopping center in Rose Hill," Brenda instructed. She would figure out later what to tell her parents.

"Hey. Okay! I'll see you then."

"Say hi to Tony for me."

"Yeah, I will. G'bye."

Brenda hung up the phone and leaned against the glass booth. She knew very well that she shouldn't really crash Laurie's party, but once the idea occurred to her there was no way she could resist. And why shouldn't she go to the bash of the year? Besides she wanted to settle things with Laurie. She just had to have the chance to say the things she should have said the first time.

Chapter
15

Dear Pheeb,

Sing your best tonight. I wish I could be there to see you. I'll send you good luck vibes at eight o'clock when I'm on the train. Do the same for me when you wake up tomorrow morning. I love you.

Brad.

Phoebe held the small card for a second and took a deep breath. Next to it was a single red rose. Brad had obviously dropped the note and the flower off in the dressing room before he left for Princeton.

Since their talk on Monday, Brad had been overly sweet and attentive. Phoebe wondered if he sensed something about Griffin, if he somehow realized that Phoebe felt something for another boy. Each day after rehearsal, Brad was waiting in the quad to drive her home. Perhaps subconsciously he knew that if she were alone with Griffin again, something would happen.

"Oh, don't be ridiculous," Phoebe said out loud, frowning into her mirror. Brad didn't even know who Griffin was.

Phoebe's corner of the small girls' dressing room was covered with cards and good luck presents. Her heart, already racing from the excitement, almost couldn't take the tension of opening even these funny little gifts. There was a homemade telegram signed by her folks and Shawn. Sasha Jenkins had sent a few of her famous granola/wheat germ cookies in a foil package tied with red ribbon. A construction paper phonograph record with Phoebe's name on it was from Peter Lacey. There was a note from Lisa apologizing that she probably couldn't make it after all. And Woody had dropped off a wrapped chocolate for each member of the cast, although Phoebe's had a special heart sticker on it.

The most meaningful present was from Chris. Fastened onto a good luck note was a small gold and pearl pin. Phoebe knew the piece of jewelry well. Chris's real mother had given it to Chris, and she always said the best things had happened to her when she had it on. For one thing, she had worn it on her first date with Ted. She rarely let the pin out of her sight, and Phoebe was very moved that her friend wanted her to wear it during the show. She slowly pushed it through the collar of her blouse and then kissed it for good luck.

There was more than an hour before the show

started, but most of the cast was backstage already. An infectious excitement and nervousness hung in the air. Everyone was laughing a little too loudly and pacing back and forth. Phoebe could hear one of the boys singing scales in the other dressing room and an occasional thud of a juggling ball hitting the floor. The girls' dressing room was alive with chatter. The smell of flowers, makeup and hair spray clouded the air. Joan Lavelle was doing ballet stretches in the far corner, while the girls from Blue Moon teased and curled their hair until they looked like they belonged in a comedy sketch from *Saturday Night Live*.

Amid all the excitement, Phoebe wondered if Griffin had arrived. Each time they sang their duet together, she felt a stronger and stronger pull toward him. And ever since she'd driven him home last week, she had found it hard to get him off her mind. During rehearsal she found herself wanting to sit near him, stand by him, always be where she could see him. But when Phoebe thought about Griffin, she also thought about Brad, and that was when her head would begin to pound.

"Not now," Phoebe whispered to herself. It was not the time to think about either Griffin or Brad. It was not the time to think about anything except the two songs she'd have to sing later that evening. She began to hum "Maybe This Time" as she looked into the old mirror in front of her. She was wearing a long forest green man's shirt over a pair of mid-calf-length culottes. A wide leather belt rested on her hips to complete the outfit. For some reason, she had also brought a favorite old green baseball cap, and was tempted to wear it.

Woody had told all the performers to wear rouge and eye makeup so that their features could be seen under the bright lights. Phoebe leaned forward and painted a rim of eye liner above and below her eyes. The liner went on like soft charcoal. She sat back critically and looked at her face. She decided she looked like one of those mummified Egyptian kings and she started to laugh.

"Joanie, is this right?" she asked the dancer, who was finishing her warm-up exercises. Joan came over and examined Phoebe's makeup.

"The line's too thick around your eyes. Other than that it's good. I have a lavender eye shadow that would be great for you. The tube is over by my tape recorder." Joanie smiled and pointed to the other end of the dressing room.

"Thanks," Phoebe said with a nod. She wiped away the eyeliner, brushed a thin coat of Joan's eye shadow just below her eyebrows and then reapplied the dark liner. She had never seen her face with so much makeup before, and she stared into the mirror, amazed at how mature she looked.

"Attention, everybody!"

It was the stage manager, Karen Carlson, standing in the doorway. She and Woody had been at the theater all afternoon getting the lights ready. She was still wearing her dirty work pants and had a hammer hanging in the loop on her hip. She looked exhausted.

"Woody wants everybody to gather backstage just before we start. Sign in so we know you're here."

Phoebe leaned forward onto the counter. Karen's voice made her realize that she was really going out there in front of her parents, her friends, and her schoolmates. That realization made her feel a little sick. Suddenly, her stomach was bouncing around like a soccer ball. She started humming and tried to relax. Then she began thinking about all the things that could possibly go wrong. She could forget the words to her song. She could open her mouth and have nothing come out. Her voice could crack — that had happened to her once during a solo in a fifth-grade choir recital. She could forget why she was even out there and just stare dumbly at the audience.

Phoebe began to laugh out loud. She realized she was living through one of her more ridiculous nightmares. Earlier that week she had actually dreamed that she was in a show like the Follies, although it was more like a school play. When she'd gone on for her big scene, she suddenly didn't know what play she was in, and she couldn't remember any of her lines. At first, Brad had been on stage with her and he seemed to know just what was going on. Later, he'd turned into Griffin. It had been very confusing, and Phoebe had woken up before she ever figured out what play she was acting in. Just remembering the dream made her feel strange.

Then Phoebe noticed one more note stuck up in the corner of the mirror. It was wedged between the frame and the glass and was almost hidden by a pair of tights which drooped down from the storage nook above. Tearing open the blue envelope, she found an antique postcard inside. It was an old-fashioned drawing of a smiling ice skater. The skater wore a long skirt and a tight-fitting jacket and hid her hands in a fur muff. On the back of the postcard was a message.

To Phoebe:
See you out on the ice. Remember, don't be afraid to fall.
Griffin.

Chris hoped she was still in time to get a good seat. She wanted Phoebe to be able to hear her applaud. She had the temptation to sneak backstage and make sure Phoebe had received her present, but Chris knew Woody wouldn't approve.

Chris had missed Phoebe all week and was secretly glad that the Follies were almost over. Things with Ted were the same — nonexistent. Life at home with Brenda was still a cold war. With Phoebe so busy at rehearsal, Chris had been lonely.

She tried not to think about it as she said hello to other kids in the Little Theater. Phoebe's brother, Shawn, a live-wire ten-year-old, was waving wildly in the doorway. Right behind him was the chubby sweet-faced Mrs. Hall and Phoebe's freckled, mustached father. The Halls waved hello to Chris, but it was getting too crowded to wade through the audience and chat.

Chris heard her name being called by a familiar voice and looked around to see who it was. Finally, she saw Sasha Jenkins up in the second row.

"Chris! I saved you a seat!" Sasha shouted above the noise. Her long, wavy hair was clipped back with wide barettes. She was motioning for Chris to come up and join her and Peter Lacey, who was sitting next to her.

Chris wove her way through the crowd until she got to the second row. Sasha and Peter were way over on the other side, but it would have been harder to get around to the other aisle than to make everyone in the row let her squeeze by. "Excuse me," Chris said politely to the first person in the row. Chris clutched her purse close to her body and began moving past on her tiptoes, trying not to step on anyone.

There wasn't much room to get by and Chris caught her foot on a stack of books that had been left on the floor. To keep from falling, she grabbed the shoulder of someone in the row in front of her. The boy she had grabbed turned instinctively, and Chris felt herself gasp. It was Ted.

He immediately stuck out his hand to help her. For a second, she just looked at him. How she had missed looking into those clear blue eyes, that open face. His hand on her bare arm sent a warm rush through her whole body.

"Hi, Chris," he said. There was something sad about his eyes, something she had never seen before.

"Hi," Chris answered shyly. It was weird to feel so awkward and timid saying hello to Ted when she really knew him so well, but that was how she felt.

They both were quiet for a moment. Then Chris noticed the girl sitting next to him. The girl turned her head to see who Ted was talking to. Chris instantly recognized freshman Danielle Du-Clos. This was the second time Chris had seen Ted with her! The sight made Chris burn.

Chris covered her hurt and anger with a brittle smile. "Excuse me," she said coldly and sidled down to the end of the row. It took every ounce of self-control for her not to look back.

"Okay, guys, you all know what you're doing. The last rehearsal was great. Just go out there and do your thing and have a great time!"

Woody was finishing his pre-show peptalk. The whole cast crowded into a small backstage room that Woody called the green room. Their collective nerves could probably have charged an electric dynamo. When he was done with his talk, they all gave him a rousing cheer.

Phoebe had come in for the tag end of Woody's speech. At the last minute, she had been hit with such a terrible case of stage fright that she'd had to go outside and get some air. When she'd made it into the green room the first person she'd spotted was Griffin.

"Where've you been? I was starting to worry about you," Griffin said excitedly. He was wearing a collarless white shirt and faded jeans with a leather patch over the back pocket. Phoebe thought he looked handsomer than she had ever seen him. He put his arm around her shoulder in a natural, easy motion.

Phoebe looked up into his face and grinned. The excitement of the show was affecting them all, and it somehow gave everyone the freedom to touch and hug. Phoebe took advantage of this and curled into Griffin. His arms wrapped around her as she relaxed against his chest. She wished she could stay there forever.

"Thanks for the card," she said at last, forcing herself to pull away. "I'm sorry I didn't get you anything."

"That's not why I gave it to you, because I wanted something back," Griffin said. His gray-blue eyes were sparkling. "Break a leg," he added with a touch to her cheek.

"You, too, Neill. See you out on the ice!"

Phoebe watched Griffin walk off to the other side of the stage. His acting sketch with Jerry Bates would be one of the first to go on. Standing in the corner beside the ropes and the old light board, Phoebe waited for the show to begin.

She got an eerie feeling when the lights went out in the audience. Suddenly everything got very quiet and the adrenaline immediately rushed through her veins.

Darrell Boldt had discovered a long tear in the side of the curtain that separated the backstage area from the stage itself, and they all hovered around it to spy on the members of the audience. Being the shortest, Phoebe was at the bottom of a row of heads all intent on seeing how the show was going over with the audience. She

170

spotted Chris, Sasha, and Peter in the second row and thought she saw Shawn toward the back.

The first few acts went well enough, but things didn't really get warmed up until Griffin and Jerry did their comic sketch. Through the slit in the curtain, Phoebe watched the audience react. Some people laughed and clapped, others sat openmouthed and fascinated. One boy on the aisle literally fell out of his chair he laughed so hard. Then, of course, the rest of the audience laughed at the boy who had fallen out of his chair. The amazing thing was that instead of ignoring the boy in the audience, Griffin included him in the sketch with a funny look and an ad lib comment. That bit of spontaneous humor earned Griffin a round of applause.

Phoebe waited nervously through Joan's dance. Her own solo was next. When she actually walked out on stage, her legs were shaking, too. Randy Nakamora played the introduction to "Maybe This Time" and Phoebe began to sing. Her voice was strong and on pitch, but she felt like someone else was singing, she was so stiff and scared. It was as if she were standing outside watching herself make each gesture like a mechanical doll. She was relieved when the song was over and she could return backstage.

Phoebe had a little time before her duet with Griffin, which was the last number of the show. She knew she hadn't messed up in her solo, but she also knew she hadn't done her best.

The other acts went by quickly. Darrell got lots of laughs for his jokes about the Kennedy teachers, Griffin's monologue was a big hit, and

Blue Moon sounded great. Phoebe's heart began to pound again as the moment for her duet got closer.

She and Griffin were to go on right after The Breakers and Poppers.

"Phoebe," whispered Griffin urgently.

Phoebe saw him next to the theater's back door. He motioned for her to join him.

"Griffin, we're on in a few minutes!"

"I know." He smiled. "I have a great idea." He whispered his idea to her, and Phoebe began to chuckle.

"Okay," she whispered back. She didn't know what it was about this boy that made her want to take such chances, but with Griffin, it seemed normal to do the extraordinary.

Clutching hands, Phoebe and Griffin slipped outside by the back door and raced around to the front of the building. They snuck in the main door and stood at the back of the auditorium. When the break dancers finished, Randy began to play the intro to "Sweet Beginnings."

Griffin walked up one aisle and Phoebe up the other. Everybody in the theater turned around to see the singers who were making such an unexpected entrance. The piano player looked especially surprised. As Phoebe walked up the aisle, she spotted Woody, who was grinning with approval.

Phoebe and Griffin answered each other's singing from different sides of the auditorium. The sensation started very slowly, but by the time they reached the stage, Phoebe felt alive and in control. She hiked herself up to sit on the edge of the stage. With a wink, Griffin jumped up next to her. They continued to sing, their voices soaring. This time, Phoebe noticed her friends in the audience, the lights, the music, everything. And she felt right at home with it all. It was like flying, like riding a perfect wave. All she wanted to do was share the fullness she felt in her heart. The song was a perfect way to do so.

As the last note faded away, a deafening cheer filled the auditorium. Phoebe and Griffin stood up and backed toward the middle of the stage. Phoebe was starting to laugh. She was so excited! Griffin grabbed her hand, and they took a bow. When she looked in his face, it was as if the two of them were the same person sharing that wonderful moment. As soon as the curtain fell, she leaped into Griffin's arms, and he swung her around and around. The spun so fast that everything else was a blur. She was only aware of the softness of Griffin's cheeks against hers and the damp warmth of his back.

"You were great!!!" Griffin yelled. Other kids from the cast were starting to pile onto the stage. Griffin let Phoebe go when the curtain went up again, and the whole cast took a group bow.

Soon, everyone was hugging and yelling. It was all over. Woody was up there, too, and he was yelling so loudly that his voice was hoarse. He spotted Phoebe and blew her a kiss. Phoebe was smiling so hard that her face hurt.

After a few moments, friends from the audience began to climb onto the stage to congratulate the performers. Phoebe's mom gave her a big hug, and Sasha promised a glowing review in the paper. Chris waited until the crowd had cleared a little before she came forward.

"Oh, Pheeb, you were wonderful. I cried during that last song, it was so beautiful," Chris sniffed. Her eyes were still damp.

"Thanks, Chris. Your pin did the trick." Phoebe beamed. "It meant a lot to me that you let me wear it. I think it brought me good luck."

Chris's eyes started to well up again and Phoebe gave her another hug. Pulling away, Chris waved good-bye, and Phoebe watched as her best friend walked out of the auditorium alone.

"Pheeberooni!" screamed Woody, "I almost died when you two came in from the back of the house, but it was a great idea. It sent chills down my spine." He looked at her lovingly. "We're all going to meet at the Sub Shop and party until we drop. Do you need a ride?"

"I have my mom's car, so I'll meet you there. It sounds great."

Phoebe finally tore herself away from the crowd and went back to the dressing room. She felt wonderful. Even her solo, though it hadn't been brilliant, was nothing to be ashamed of. Somehow, being so scared and still going on and getting through it had made a special experience for her. And the duet! Phoebe had known that was great from the moment it started.

She gathered her notes and presents in her bag and said good-bye to the other girls. She was hot and a little sweaty from all the excitement as she stepped out the back door to cool off. She leaned against the outside wall and looked up at the clear, star-filled sky. It was truly a gorgeous night.

A figure was silhouetted in the light of the doorway, and Phoebe sensed instantly that it was Griffin. His long legs, strong frame, and proud stance were so familiar to her by now. He walked slowly over to her and leaned next to her on the wall, their shoulders touching.

"What a night," Phoebe sighed happily.

"Yeah, what a night," Griffin repeated, looking up at the sky.

Phoebe hesitated for a moment. "Are you going to the Sub Shop?"

Griffin shrugged. "What are you doing?"

Phoebe looked down at the ground. Griffin knew Brad was away in Princeton and wouldn't be back until tomorrow. She closed her eyes and bit her bottom lip.

Finally Griffin spoke. "Maybe you and I should just go out by ourselves."

Phoebe was unable to answer for a moment. Going out alone with Griffin was what she wanted to do more than anything in the world. And yet, she knew she shouldn't. That would be cheating on Brad. She knew she would be letting herself go too far.

"Well," Griffin said softly. "Do you want to?"

Phoebe opened her eyes and turned slowly toward him. There was a slant of light over his brow, but the rest of his face was in the shadows. When he stepped closer, she had no desire to move back.

Before she knew it, he was kissing her. It happened so easily, so naturally. They came together at the same time, gently, tenderly. Griffin placed his hands tightly around her back and she rested her arms over his shoulders. She felt like she was swimming in a pool of sun, of warmth, of love.

They relaxed in each other's embrace. Then, slowly, they pulled apart.

"Come on," Phoebe breathed.

Hand in hand, they ran across the dark quad as fast as they could, unaware of anything but each other.

Chapter 16

It was a perfect night. The sky was clear, and each star was bursting with its own brilliant light. A sweet, even wind blew the piles of dried leaves, making them rise and swirl. Each time a gust came up, it brought with it just a hint of chill.

Phoebe leaned back and took off her baseball cap. She wanted to feel the wind blowing through her heavy mane of hair. Resting her head back, she closed her eyes and let the breeze tumble over her like a wave.

Griffin stood a few feet in front of her. His arms were stretched up to the sky. The back of his shirt was untucked and billowing in the wind. He felt that if he reached a little higher, he might just sail off into the heavens.

But the last thing Griffin wanted was to sail off. He didn't want to be anywhere other than where he was. Right now, he felt like he was in exactly the right place at exactly the right time.

He knew that his performance had gone extraordinarily well. He had felt his talent, his power over the audience, the joy that had passed between him and those who had watched. And then there was Phoebe. At last, he was with the one girl who meant as much to him as being up on stage.

They both looked down as far as they could along the old railroad tracks. Other than the sound of the wind, it was quiet, and the only light was from the few yellow overhead lamps.

"What do you think?" asked Griffin with a mischievous smile on his handsome face.

"I think you're right." Phoebe beamed. "This is one of the best places in Rose Hill. I can't believe I've never been here."

Phoebe began to wander around the outside of the old railroad station. It must once have been the center of Rose Hill, but now it was run-down and neglected. Still, there was something charming and romantic about it. The station was a barnlike building painted a dark green. It still had ornate decorations carved in the window and door frames, although one pane of glass was bandaged with heavy strips of tape. A dim light had been left on inside, exposing a cluttered desk and a stack of cardboard boxes. The platform was a huge wooden rectangle that bordered the deeply cut track. In spite of the ghostly quality of the place, it was mysterious and beautiful.

"Look out at the track," urged Griffin. "Can't you just imagine that it's a hundred years ago? All you have to do is block out the tops of the buildings on the other side. It could be the early 1900s."

Phoebe could picture it instantly. She envisioned huge puffs of steam as the shiny train rolled into the station, women arriving on the long wooden platform wearing floor-length traveling suits and lace-up boots. They must have looked like the skater on Griffin's postcard. They would have been carrying hat boxes and clutching the hands of children in knickers and tweed caps. Phoebe could almost hear the call of the conductor.

"Why don't the trains come here anymore?" she asked.

Griffin walked over to her. "They do, but they don't carry people now, just freight. Don't you hear the whistle at night?"

Phoebe shook her head no.

"Really? I guess you can't hear it way over on your side of town. You sure can hear it over here. I love the sound. Sometimes, when I lie in bed at night, I wait for that whistle and let it put me to sleep."

Phoebe looked into Griffin's face. He had that wonderful dreamy, excited look again. His arm fell over her shoulder, and she felt a pleasant warmth. She let her arm lace under his and gave his narrow waist a squeeze. The cotton of his shirt was cool against her cheek.

"It's so beautiful here," she whispered.

"I was hoping you'd like it." He smiled. "It's one of the great unappreciated places in Rose Hill."

For a moment, they were quiet. Phoebe could hear a dog barking off in the distance. She could feel the rough edge of Griffin's denim waistband against her hand. The lamp behind them created long, elegant shadows, and she could just see the healthy pink of Griffin's cheeks.

Griffin began to smooth his hand over Phoebe's back in a slow, graceful pattern. She continued to look out at the horizon, but she found it hard to think about anything except the feeling of his hand against her spine. She almost felt as if she were spinning, as if nothing existed but that one part of her body. When she turned to face Griffin, he was already looking at her.

This time, when he looked at her with that intense gaze, she knew just what it meant and just how to respond. She felt the same way he did — she wanted to see him as deeply as possible, to look into his soul if she could. It was impossible to think of anything but him and being in this strange, magical place.

Phoebe lifted her face and Griffin kissed her slowly, lightly on the mouth. Again and again he kissed her until she felt almost as if she couldn't breathe. She pulled away for a moment and rested her head on his chest. Griffin's heart was pounding.

She hugged him hard, then relaxed in his arms. His neck was warm and soft and she felt his fine hair brush along her mouth. His touch seemed to echo throughout her body. They began to kiss again, this time more deeply and passionately.

"Phoebe, I love you," Griffin said in a breathy voice, his body shaking.

For a moment, Phoebe wasn't sure if he had really said it or not. She clasped her hands even tighter around his neck and felt his breath along the side of her ear. He said it again, and Phoebe felt like she was floating in a cloud of cotton. But a second later an alarm went off inside her head.

She wanted to say "I love you" back, but she couldn't. She knew she had already gone over the line. Here she was, alone with Griffin, holding him, kissing him. And the way she was feeling, she knew she was in love with him — more in love than she had ever been in her life. But saying those words was impossible. It was as if Brad were listening somewhere. Brad was the only boy she had ever said those words to — or heard them from. Listening to them come from another boy cut through Phoebe's joy and forced her to remember that there was someone else involved in her life. That someone wasn't enjoying the romantic old railroad station and the beautiful night but was in Princeton, New Jersey, innocently sleeping and worrying about nothing but his interview the next day.

Phoebe broke away from Griffin and walked over to an old bench that leaned along the station wall. Griffin followed her and crouched on the ground.

Phoebe leaned forward and rested her head in her hands. "What am I going to do?" she pleaded.

"Just do what you feel," urged Griffin.

Phoebe shook his head. "What am I going to do about Brad?"

Finally, she had said it. In all the time she and

Griffin had been together, at rehearsal, when she drove him home, every second there had been a tension and an attraction. Brad had been the ghost who stood between them. Certainly, he had been on both of their minds. But since the first time Griffin had asked who Brad was, his name had not been mentioned. At last, they had to talk about the main obstacle to their relationship.

Griffin squeezed Phoebe's hand. "Do you love Brad?" he asked slowly.

Phoebe took a moment. She pictured Brad's sturdy straightforward face. Of course she loved him. Brad was like a part of her family, like her father or Shawn. She had been with him for two whole years. Over that time they had shared so many things. Seeing the serious look in Griffin's eyes, Phoebe knew she had an important decision to make.

"Yes, I love Brad," she said. She could feel Griffin's hands tense. "But I'm not in love with him. Not anymore."

His hand relaxed. "Do you still want to go out with him?" Griffin said these words carefully.

Phoebe pulled back her hands and put her palms over her eyes. Suddenly, she wished she would hear that old train whistle and see the engine pull into the station. She and Griffin would get on it and travel somewhere away from to-morrow, away from the unpleasantness of the real world. "It just doesn't seem fair to him. Here you and I are together, and he has no idea. It's just not fair!"

"What's not fair is to be with someone you don't love. It's not fair to you or to him," Griffin reasoned. He made Phoebe lift her head. "But I do know that what I feel for you is very strong. So strong that there just can't be anything unfair or bad about it."

Phoebe looked at Griffin for a moment, then rushed suddenly into his arms. He held her close and kissed her on the forehead. She didn't know she was crying until she felt the wetness spilling down her cheeks. Griffin wiped the first of her tears away and hugged her even closer.

"It's okay," he whispered.

Something about his words made Phoebe burst into a full sob. Her tears flowed freely coming from a deeper place than she'd even known existed. Unashamed, she let her sobs burst out and did not try to hold back. At last, Phoebe realized, she knew where that old fizzy, exploding feeling had come from. It was all the fear and frustration she had been holding inside for so long. All those times she had pushed down her feelings to please someone else. All those times she had settled for following someone else's path instead of finding her own.

When it was over and she calmed down, she wiped away the tears, the trails of makeup and broke into a tiny smile. Her body felt drained, as if she had just run a cross-country race. She begun to realize what a long day it had been.

"What are you going to do?" Griffin asked finally.

Phoebe looked up at the stars. It had to be after midnight. A half-moon looked down on her from high up in the sky. Her nose was still running.

"I'm not sure," she said, shivering slightly. "I guess I should wait until Brad comes home tomorrow night. He deserves to know what's going on."

Griffin put his hands on her shoulders. "Yes, but remember, it's not going to be easy. The main thing is to do what you feel and then go with it one hundred percent. There's no point in staying with someone just to be nice. In the end, that will just hurt Brad even more. You might not get that many chances in your life to really be in love. You have to grab the opportunity when it comes along or it will disappear!"

Phoebe looked into Griffin's intense face and wondered if she were made to take the kind of chances he was asking of her. Part of her wanted to shout her love for him at the top of her voice, not to worry about the consequences. But part of her was too scared and too sensible to go out on that limb. Part of her wanted to think things over before she acted, to plan and make sure she was making the right choice.

Not too far off, a train whistle blew three times. Phoebe gulped and got up. She ran to the edge of the platform, the tension of the past few minutes easing as she moved. Sure enough, in the distance, she saw the large single light of an oncoming train. The whistle hooted again. It was hollow and high and seemed to scream with the same kind of confusion she felt inside.

Griffin ran up beside her. "Listen, isn't that a great sound!" They began to trot together along the edge of the platform.

"Yes!!!" Phoebe yelled, enjoying the freedom

of her own voice. "Will it stop here?"

Griffin looked at the train again. It was quite a bit closer. "I don't think so, since there's no one here."

"There's something I've always been dying to do," Phoebe shouted. The roar of the train was getting louder and the whistle blew one more time.

She grabbed Griffin's hand and pulled him back over to the bench. Standing on top of it, she motioned for Griffin to climb up next to her. They stood and listened as the sound of the train grew louder and louder, speeding toward the station.

As the headlight rushed closer, Phoebe put her fingers in her ears and Griffin looked at her with a curious smile. At last, the engine pulled in with an immense roar and Phoebe began to yell with all her might — a free, uninhibited wail. Instantly, Griffin joined her screams as the train sped noisily by. They couldn't even hear each other but they continued to sing and yell with all their might. They didn't stop shrieking until the caboose rumbled away from the station.

Phoebe and Griffin sank down onto the bench. "I've always imagined doing that," Phoebe laughed. Her throat felt hoarse and raw.

"It's a good thing we won't have to sing for a while." Griffin grinned. His voice was also raspy and weak. With a low, relaxed chuckle he started to laugh and threw his arms around Phoebe, resting his head on her shoulder. She clutched his hands laughing and sighing all at once.

Finally, Phoebe turned to hug Griffin, her face

meeting his. All her anxiety and indecision had been screamed away. Her fear had run off like some nerveless ghost. Once again Phoebe was full of happiness and love — so full that she felt ready to burst. Not the old painful, anxious kind of bursting, but a warm sensation that filled her every pore. She had no idea what the future would bring, but this, she decided, was the best night of her life.

Chapter
17

When Phoebe woke up the next morning, she couldn't believe that everything around her looked the same. She felt so different. But her room was still painted pale blue, the yellow teddy bear still sat on the window seat, the *Chorus Line* poster Woody had brought her from New York still hung above her desk. Outside her window, nothing had changed either. Through the slats in the shutters, Phoebe could see that the front lawn was as green as ever. Her mom's station wagon was parked in the circular front driveway. Shawn's ten-speed still sprawled against the huge oak tree.

Phoebe looked at her alarm clock and sat upright with a shock. It was after eleven o'clock! Brad's interview was certainly over by now. Not only had she forgotten to send him good luck, she had slept through it all without a thought. Phoebe had never been drunk, but she felt the way people looked in movies when they had a hangover. Her head was heavy and her stomach raw. She could still feel the scraping in her throat from screaming the night before with the train. It was all coming back to her. She hugged her pillow fiercely.

There was a soft knock on her door.

Phoebe cleared her throat. "Come in."

Her mother came into the doorway and flicked on the light switch. Phoebe squinted and tried to smile.

Mrs. Hall came over and sat on the edge of the bed. Curls of light brown hair framed her round face. She put the inside of her wrist on Phoebe's forehead. "Honey, do you feel all right?"

"Uh huh." Phoebe sat up straighter.

"I thought you were going to sleep all day." She picked the quilted bedspread up off the floor and sat back down. "Your father and I heard you come in last night. It was after one."

Phoebe looked away. She knew her parents never fell asleep until they were sure she was in the house. She hoped they would relax her midnight curfew just this once.

"Sorry," Phoebe said.

"I know it was a big night for you and that you were out celebrating with your friends."

Phoebe felt a tinge of relief. Her mom didn't seem very mad or upset.

Mrs. Hall pushed up the sleeves of her velour shirt. "We're not going to make a big deal about it this time, but if it happens again, you are going to be grounded."

Phoebe looked down at her lap. "Okay."

"We worry about you when we don't know where you are."

"I know."

Mrs. Hall smiled and brushed back Phoebe's hair. "We decided to go up and stay at the cabin tonight." Phoebe's family owned a small cabin in the mountains. Her father loved to go up there to relax. "After last night, your father was going to insist that you come with us, but I know you have a party with your friends. If I leave you here alone, do you promise to be home early and act responsibly?"

Phoebe scratched her head and smiled. "Of course, Mom. Last night was just special. I promise not to do it again. You know you can trust me."

"I know that, but your father is not so sure. We can call Mrs. Beecham and ask her to stay with you."

"Mom, that's dumb. I can take care of things, you know that. And I promise I won't be out late again tonight." Phoebe thought about Laurie's party and wondered when Brad would get back from Princeton. "Did Brad call this morning?" she asked suddenly.

Her mom got up and opened the shutters. The early afternoon sun was painfully bright. "No, dear. Don't worry. I'm sure he did just fine."

Phoebe nodded and pushed back the covers. Somehow, that was not what she was worried about.

"Honey, I managed to save you a Danish. It's hiding in the cookie jar — that is, if Shawn hasn't discovered it yet. We're leaving soon, and we should be back by dinnertime tomorrow. Okay?"

"Sure." Phoebe smiled and got up to give her mom a hug. She kissed her on the cheek. "Thanks a lot."

Her mom returned the kiss. "By the way," she said on her way out, "we were very proud of you in the show last nght." With a wink, Mrs. Hall padded off toward the kitchen.

Phoebe waited until her mom disappeared down the hall. She slumped back onto the edge of her bed and rubbed her temples. Now that she was awake, her problems all came flooding back into her thoughts. What a mess she was in over Griffin and Brad. Soon, she would have to make a decision and do something about it. That was not a moment she was looking forward to.

After Shawn and her folks left for the mountains, Phoebe changed into her jogging clothes. Exercise would help her think more clearly. Besides, she wanted to return Chris's pin. Since her parents had taken the station wagon and she wasn't allowed to drive her father's Audi, she had no choice other than to jog.

In her red sweat pants and blue-and-white baseball shirt, Phoebe ran over to see Chris. She held the pin in her hand so that she wouldn't lose it. Her hair, pulled back in a ponytail high on her head, swished back and forth along her neck as she ran. She still felt a little tired, but her eyes were open wide.

When Phoebe reached the slope before Chris's house, she felt a slight cramp in her side and slowed to a walk. It was cool and overcast. A tiny patch of sun peeked through on the other side of the sky, and Phoebe wondered if that tiny bit of brightness was shining on Griffin. Her cramp gradually eased, and she hopped up the steps to Chris's front door lightly.

Mr. Austin answered. Formal and erect, he was the only person Phoebe had ever seen who had better posture than Chris. Even though it was Saturday, he wore a pressed shirt and slacks. Unlike her own father, who almost never shaved on weekends, Mr. Austin was smooth-faced and smelled of pine.

"Come in, Phoebe," he said graciously. He motioned her in and closed the door, then he showed her to the kitchen where Mrs. Austin and Brenda were eating lunch in the corner breakfast nook. Brenda didn't look up when Phoebe said hello.

"Chris is in the backyard," Mrs. Austin said in her refined voice. Phoebe thanked her and went to the wide wooden door that led out back.

The Austins' backyard was divided into two sections. The first was a square which, in the summer, was filled with a table and lawn chairs. Around the side, a blacktopped square faced the side of the garage. It was hedged by a row of tall bushes, and there was a basketball hoop attached to the roof. Phoebe knew that this was where Mr. Austin spent hour after hour shooting baskets. Sometimes Chris played with him. Once, Phoebe had been talked into playing with them, but she had giggled so much and shot so poorly that she had never been asked again.

Today, Chris was standing near the fence that ran along the back of the blacktopped square. She was hitting a tennis ball against the garage wall with angry concentration. Her blond hair was braided, and she wore a white T-shirt and shorts. Her concentration was so fierce that she reminded Phoebe of a tennis pro playing the match of her life. She didn't notice her friend until the ball bounced off in Phoebe's direction. Phoebe stepped in to catch the stray ball and tossed it back to Chris.

"Hi!" Chris was surprised, but very glad to see her. She set down her racket, peeled the white terry cloth bands off her wrists and gave Phoebe a quick hug. "You were so good last night in the Follies! I thought you were the very best!"

"Oh, thanks." Phoebe shrugged with embarrassment. "I think it was your pin that did it."

Phoebe held out the pin, and Chris took it back with a wistful smile. She fastened it onto the waistband of her shorts.

"Are you going to Laurie's party tonight?" Chris asked.

"I guess."

Phoebe couldn't imagine sitting home alone. At least at Laurie's party she would have company while waiting for Brad to get back. "Are you?"

Chris tossed the tennis ball against the garage wall and batted it like a handball. "I said I would. I just hope Ted's not with Danielle DuClos again. I don't know if I could handle that." She slapped the ball hard, and it bounced back to the far corner.

Phoebe walked over to fetch it. She had forgotten about Ted and Danielle.

"I don't really think Ted is serious about her." Phoebe wasn't just saying it to make Chris feel better. She was sure that freshman Danielle wasn't Ted's type at all.

"He was at the Follies with her."

"Still, from you to Danielle is quite a leap. I don't think he likes her."

Phoebe tossed the ball back to Chris.

Chris bounced the ball as hard as she could on the ground and watched it shoot up high. Finally, she caught it and set it down on her racket. "Anyway, I'm going to Laurie's party." Chris wiped her forehead. "How was your cast party last night? Woody said you were all going out to the Sub Shop. He invited me to come, but I just wasn't up to it."

Phoebe couldn't hold it in any longer. If there was one person she wanted to talk to, it was Chris. That was why she'd come here. Phoebe flopped over at the waist and put her hands on her knees. She lifted her head. "I have to talk to you, Chris," she said in a low voice.

"Wait, let's go inside."

Phoebe followed Chris back through the living room and up the oak stairway. Silently, Chris shut the door to her bedroom, checking it once to make sure it was really closed. They both sat cross-legged on one of the beds.

"What's the matter?" Chris folded her hands

in her lap. Her pale eyebrows were knitted with concern.

Phoebe didn't know how to begin. She had carried this secret for so long, it was strange suddenly to talk about it. Figuring that the most direct way was the best, she began. "I've fallen in love."

The two girls sat there for a moment facing each other. Chris was so puzzled that she didn't know what to say.

"What?"

"I'm in love," Phoebe repeated.

"You mean with Brad?" Chris looked more confused than before.

Phoebe shook her head and her ponytail rocked from side to side. "No."

"Then who?"

Phoebe looked up at the ceiling. "With Griffin Neill."

"Griffin Neill? The guy from the Follies? The one you sang with?" Her face was still a picture of confusion.

"Yes."

"But I don't understand. When did this happen?"

"Last night."

Phoebe waited through a long pause. Chris was obviously shocked. "I mean, not really last night. Really, it's been going on since I met him, since I auditioned for the Follies. There have been some incredibly strong feelings between us. But we didn't do anything about them until last night."

Chris's mouth hung open wide. "Didn't you go to the cast party?"

Phoebe shook her head. "No, I went out with Griffin, alone." As if she couldn't stop talking, Phoebe told Chris all about what had happened between her and Griffin. She told her about the railroad station and kissing him and the way he'd told her he loved her. Chris listened silently and looked down at the bedspread. "Chris, what am I going to do? I've never felt like this before."

Finally Chris lifted her head. "What about Brad?"

Phoebe drew her knees under her and leaned forward. "I'm not in love with him anymore."

"When did you decide that? The day Brad went away to Princeton?" There was an edge in Chris's voice.

"No. I don't know. I guess I didn't realize it until then or something. It's all very confusing, Chris."

"After two years, you suddenly decide that you're in love with someone else who you barely know?"

"I guess, but Chris. . . ."

Chris sat up very straight. "Does Brad know anything about this?"

"No."

"So he doesn't even know that anything is wrong?"

"Uh-uh."

"How can you do this to him? It's so unfair."

"I know. I know!" Phoebe pounded the bed with her fist. Chris was beginning to make her feel really awful.

195

"Why didn't you break up with Brad if you felt that way about somebody else?"

"Because, I don't know, I didn't know I felt this way. And now, I don't know what to do or how to do it."

"Phoebe, Brad totally trusts you. I'm sorry, but what you did was wrong."

Phoebe stood up and looked at Chris. Suddenly, her best friend's perfect features and even blond hair made her angry. How could someone who looked so beautiful on the outside be so insensitive underneath. Even if Chris were right, it didn't matter. What Phoebe wanted was friendship and support, not a lecture on how badly she'd handled her love life.

"Chris, I can't believe you're saying this to me?"

"Why?"

"Because you're my best friend and you're supposed to make me feel better and tell me that things are going to be okay. Instead you're just making me feel worse!"

"Oh, so because I'm your friend I'm supposed to lie to you and tell you you've done something great when you just betrayed the guy you've been going out with for two years. Is that what a best friend is supposed to do?"

Phoebe's jaw clenched. "I don't think you really know what a best friend is or what friendship is. If you don't watch it, you may just end up with no friends at all!"

Phoebe and Chris stared at each other, then Phoebe opened the bedroom door with an angry sweep and walked into the hall and down the stairs without looking right or left. She was half-way home before she noticed anything around her.

After Phoebe left, Chris fell onto the bed and curled up facing the wall. She had tried to sound tactful and kind. She had even been right. She knew she had been right! But what did that matter when she had just lost her best friend? What did anything matter without Ted, without Phoebe? She heard her stepmother laugh downstairs, and a second later Brenda's husky voice joined in.

Chris pulled a pillow in to her stomach to try to ease the empty, hollow feeling she had inside. She would never forget that look of hurt in Phoebe's face, the hurt that she had caused. Something else was over. That was all she could think. Something else was over.

Chapter
18

"Sheila, don't put those potato chips there!"

Laurie Bennington was having a hard time dealing with the help. The usual cook and housekeeper weren't sufficient for the kind of party Laurie had planned, so her parents agreed to hire a caterer. The only thing was, Laurie hadn't expected a caterer who happened to be such a klutz. Potato chips on the mantelpiece just wasn't done in the Bennington household.

"And I want that tablecloth to be spread diagonally," Laurie instructed, "with the pattern showing this way."

Would she ever get everything straightened out in time? True, she was dressed, made up, blow dried and perfumed, but she still wasn't quite certain if this was exactly what she wanted to wear. She had left three outfits hanging in her closet, ready for a quick change should that be necessary. Still Laurie was wishing she felt more reassured. What if her party were a failure? What if Peter didn't show up at all?

Laurie told herself to stay calm. There was much to suggest that things really were going to go her way. The kitchen was packed with trays of artistically arranged finger-sized hotdogs, egg rolls, chips, and dips. The caterer had done her best, and the housekeeper had loaded the refrigerator with cases of soda and bags of ice. At exactly nine o'clock, Mario's would be delivering over a dozen deluxe pizzas. The front and backyard trees had been decorated with lanterns and strings of lights. Inside, the decorations followed a rock'n'roll theme, with posters and photos that Mr. Bennington had brought home from one of his television stations. It was nearly perfect.

And there was more. Laurie gloated over the collection of rock videos her father had managed to get for her. Some of them had not even been on television yet. The housekeeper and Laurie's mother had set up the video player and rearranged the living room furniture to turn it into a mini movie theater. There was a special corner for Peter. Laurie placed two chairs next to her father's state-of-the-art stereo and video systems. One was for Peter when he was changing records. The other, of course, was for her. She could hardly wait.

Luckily, the weather was mild and dry. Laurie stepped out to the backyard and turned on the string of lights that hung from the trees surrounding the swimming pool. It looked like a carnival. A slight breeze made tiny ripples in the water and rustled through the landscaped greenery.

Laurie smiled as she noticed how the pale moonlight made her red silk dress glisten. The dress was from Rezato, the chicest boutique in Georgetown, and had cost a bundle. It had a wide neck that tended to slide off one shoulder, a sashed waist, and a slit that reached from the hem to her mid-thigh. Even from her blurry reflection in the water, Laurie could tell she looked sensational.

Still, was it exactly the right outfit? Maybe. Everything was set up just right. Her parents had promised to leave before the party started and stay out until late. The most popular kids in school were all coming, and tomorrow everyone at Kennedy would know Laurie Bennington had thrown the party of the year. And that Laurie and Peter Lacey were now madly in love.

When Chris arrived just after nine, she had to wait for the pizza man to bring in his endless supply of pizzas before she walked in. Actually, Chris wasn't so sure anymore why she had come. The first car she had spotted coming up the street had been Ted's MG. Just the sight of the tiny red sports car had made her want to cry. She realized she was even wearing the same pale blue sweater and white pleated pants she had worn on her first date with him.

As soon as Chris walked into Laurie's house, she saw Phoebe standing in the front of the living room. She had almost walked right into her. She tried to get by without Phoebe seeing her, but it was impossible. John Marquette backed up against her — making some rude comment while he was doing it — and Chris was forced to come face to face with Phoebe. For a long moment, the two girls glared at each other until Phoebe angrily stormed off toward the kitchen. Chris felt like she was sinking.

She heard Ted's voice coming from the far corner, but she put her head down so she wouldn't have to see him. She didn't want to embarrass herself by bursting into tears in the middle of the party. Yet she felt that pressure building up behind her eyes and in her throat. She tried to hold her eyes open wide and smile — anything to hold back the loneliness she felt inside.

At last, Chris saw a safe, friendly face. It was Peter Lacey, and he was in the corner, playing with the expensive stereo. It was the opposite corner from where Ted was, so Chris pushed through the crowd of kids to say hello.

Peter looked up and smiled brightly. "Hi, kid." He patted her on the hand and went right back to the row of buttons under the turntable. "This is a truly amazing system." He shook his head in appreciation and turned up the volume. The beat pounded even louder in Chris's head. When Chris put her hands over his ears, he leaned in and turned it back down.

"Too loud for you?"

Chris smiled sadly.

"Sorry. Hey, you okay?"

Chris tried to be upbeat. "Sure."

Peter looked at her and winked. "You want to help me set up the video machine?"

Chris started to laugh. Peter's expression was so excited and sweet, as if setting up the video machine would be a great way to cheer her up.

"No, thanks," she answered and gave him a playful punch in the arm. "I think I need some air."

"Okay." Peter nodded. He pushed a lock of hair out of his eyes. "Maybe you need to sit alone for a few minutes. If you need a friend, you know where to find me."

"Thanks." Still trying to hold back her sadness, Chris made her way to the back part of the house.

When Phoebe went into the kitchen she was very happy to find Woody and Sasha perched up on the counter. They had a steaming pizza between them and were about to attack it.

"Want some?" Sasha asked happily. She was picking the pieces of pepperoni off one piece of the pie.

"No, thanks," said Phoebe. "I guess I'm not too hungry." She smiled at Woody and hopped up on the counter next to him, pausing a minute to lean her head on his arm.

It wasn't the thing to do. Woody tensed up when Phoebe touched him and almost moved away. When he looked at her, there was hurt in his eyes. Instead of greeting her in his usual energetic way, he stared down at his high-topped red sneakers and nervously kicked his feet together.

Phoebe was very surprised by Woody's unfriendly reaction. If she could count on anyone for friendship, even adoration, it was always Woody. She tried to ignore his coldness and hoped it wasn't due to something she'd done. "Isn't there a plain pizza?" she asked Sasha. Vegetarian Sasha was now carefully removing all the sausage.

"Nope. Laurie went all out and ordered only Mario's super specials. Gross."

Without even waiting for his slice of pizza, Woody jumped down off the counter and walked purposefully away into the living room. Phoebe watched his wiry form, his step much heavier than usual. One of the clips of his suspenders was hangng loose in back, and it flapped against his hip.

Phoebe turned to Sasha, who was trying to keep her long hair from trailing onto her slice of pizza as she took the first, gooey bite. "Sasha, is Woody mad at me about something?"

Sasha put down her food and wiped her mouth with a personalized Bennington napkin. She gave Phoebe a sympathetic look. "He's mad about the party after the Follies last night. He was hurt that you didn't come."

"Great." Phoebe sighed. She had totally forgotten about Woody and the cast party.

"He thinks you and that guy Griffin Neill went out alone," Sasha said quietly. "I suppose he's just jealous that you might like Griffin." Sasha picked up her pizza and began eating again.

Phoebe put her head down, and her thick hair fell around her face. She didn't know if she could take Woody being mad at her.

"Why is he jealous? Woody and I are just friends. I've been with Brad forever, and Woody's never been jealous of him."

"Don't worry." Sasha patted Phoebe's shoulder. "Woody has always been so crazy about you, but I think he just accepted you dating Brad as the way it is. But if you broke up with Brad for somebody else, and that somebody else wasn't him, I think he would feel hurt for a little while."

"I haven't broken up with Brad," Phoebe said defensively. She didn't want another lecture like the one from Chris. Sasha smiled softly, and Phoebe realized that, of all people, she would be the last one to pass judgment on her.

"I'm just telling you what Woody told me before you got here." She finished off the cheesy part of her slice and left the crust on her paper plate. She licked her fingers carefully. "Don't let it upset you. Sometimes I think Woody enjoys it this way. I mean, he always likes girls who already have boyfriends. He'll forgive you in a day or two. I'm sure he will. He knows you would never hurt him intentionally. Just leave him alone, and in a little while it will be as though it never happened."

Phoebe sighed. She was very glad Sasha was so supportive because she didn't think she could take someone else being down on her.

Laurie appeared in the doorway. She looked very dramatic in her red dress and, from the excited look on her face, everything was going just the way she'd hoped.

"We're going to show some videos very soon. You'd better come in if you want a good seat," Laurie crooned.

Sasha and Phoebe looked at each other and shrugged. They hopped down off the counter and followed Laurie into the living room.

By now, the living room was packed with kids. Many were dancing to Peter's record selections, and Phoebe recognized a few honor kids, a few jocks, most of the student body officers — basically anybody who was somebody at Kennedy. Ted was in the corner trying to talk to two other football players over the loud music. When he spotted Phoebe, he waved warmly and came over to join her.

"Phoebe!" he cheered and gave her a short hug. He looked as handsome as ever in a red sweater and jeans, but that old sparkle was gone from his eyes. He was obviously attending the party alone.

"When's Brad getting back?" he asked as he looked around the room. Phoebe wondered if he was looking for Chris.

Phoebe flushed. For a moment, she didn't know what to say. "Later tonight, I guess." She stuck her hands in her pockets.

"How'd he do in his interview? Did you talk to him?"

Again Phoebe felt uneasy. "No, not yet. I'm sure he did great." Suddenly, she couldn't look Ted in the eye.

"Uh, Pheeb . . ." Ted trailed off.

"Yes. What?"

"Where did Chris go to? I saw her come in, but I think maybe she went home or something." He shifted his shoulders uncomfortably.

Phoebe looked around. She didn't see Chris either. Maybe Chris had decided to go on home.

"I don't know where she is," Phoebe said sadly. "She and I are kind of on the outs."

Ted looked surprised and seemed about to ask Phoebe more, when a rush of kids flooded the living room, making it impossible to continue any private conversation. Peter was in the corner setting up the video equipment. Laurie came in and struck a dramatic pose. "It's time to put on some extra special videos," she announced. Then she took her seat next to him and gave him a huge, flirtatious smile, right in front of everybody. All the guests found seats as the lights went down and the tapes came on.

Chris had tried everything. She'd hidden in the basement, the bathroom, and Laurie's bedroom. Eventually, she'd been discovered in every place. Trying to look nonchalant coming out of Laurie's "boudoir," as the housekeeper called it, was worst of all. Big deal, though. The housekeeper couldn't send to her jail. Laurie probably wouldn't like it, but she was so busy flirting with poor Peter she probably wouldn't even notice if the roof caved in.

She'd finally ended up in the backyard. At least it was quiet out there and she could look at the lights shining peacefully on the swimming pool. She was hidden by a big tree, but she could still see the flicker on the video screen inside the house. Ted was in there. Phoebe too. All of them probably wondering where she'd gone. Or maybe she was just flattering herself. Maybe they didn't care at all. Chris thought about it, then sat down firmly on the Bennington diving board.

It was scratchy, rough. Even through the soles of her flat shoes she could feel that plastic stuff that helps your feet keep their grip until you're finally ready to jump off. Keeping a grip on things, that was exactly Chris's problem. She hadn't been able to keep a grip on her anger at Ted or her moralizing with Phoebe. "Old Chris Austin, the champion high diver," Chris muttered bitterly to herself. "She tries to do a perfect double flip, but she ends up doing one big belly flop."

No one heard her. Everyone was having too much fun inside. Everybody but dumb, silly, open-your-mouth-wide-and-say-something-unforgivable Chris. Ohhh! Why had she even come? Why had she decided to punish herself this way? She was just dragging people down. Nobody wanted her here.

Chris hunched over atop the diving board in a posture of complete and utter despair.

Chapter 19

Brenda had no trouble finding Laurie's house. It was only a few blocks from her own, and it was the biggest and showiest in the neighborhood. But when she, Danny, and Ray pulled up in Ray's old Chevy, she started to have second thoughts. Staring out the window at the cars lining the block, Brenda wondered if crashing Laurie's party wasn't one of her all-time terrible ideas.

"Is that the house? Wow," said Ray in a slow drawl.

He was an eighteen-year-old from the country who had arrived at the halfway house a few days before. He had freckles and big ears and one of the weirdest laughs Brenda had ever heard. He smoked Camel cigarettes nonstop and he kept calling Brenda "the little lady." He also drove very fast and tried to prove to Brenda and Danny that he was a great driver by telling them he knew how to double-clutch when going fast around corners. Unlike most of the kids at the halfway house, who just had problems, Ray was a real loser.

With the car stopped in the middle of the street, Ray stuck his head out the window and ogled the Bennington house. "Those folks must have quite a bundle."

"Hey, Ray, park or something. We're blocking traffic," Danny complained in an annoyed voice. He was also beginning to regret having asked this strange, tall kid to join them.

"Yeah, Ray. Don't stop in the middle of the street," Brenda urged.

Brenda wished Ray would disappear. Even though Danny dressed a little like a hood in his T-shirt and sleeveless denim vest, he was a bright guy. He knew how to act in any situation and was sensible and considerate. But this Ray kid, there was no telling what he was capable of.

"Maybe we should forget it and go to a movie," said Brenda.

"Naah, I like it here, little lady," objected Ray. He stepped on the gas pedal and sped halfway down the block to a parking place.

Brenda and Danny looked at each other.

"What do you want to do, Bren?" Danny asked.

Brenda thought for a moment. She had a decision to make. It was dangerous to get near the Bennington home with creepy Ray tagging along, but she still wanted to get her feelings about Laurie off her chest, the way the psychology book had suggested. She decided she should just go to the front door, tell Laurie Bennington that she was a human being whose feelings mattered, and then split right away.

"How about if you two wait here. I just want to go in for a second and then I'll be right back. Okay?"

"Sure," agreed Danny.

"Hey, yeah," drawled Ray as he slammed his car door and walked around to the trunk, rolling a Camel unfiltered between his fingers. He banged on the trunk with his fist and it sprang open. Reaching in with his long, skinny arm, he pulled out a bottle of vodka. In one movement, he unscrewed the top and took a generous swig.

Right away, Danny tried to grab the bottle, but Ray lifted it high and Danny was too short to reach. Ray laughed a slow, dumb chuckle. Danny was about to try again, but Brenda stopped him.

"If he really wants to mess himself up, there's no way you can stop him. Just get the car keys. You should drive home, Danny. I'll be right back and then we'll go over to Garfield House."

"That's right, little lady, you tell him. Ol' Ray here is going to have himself a good time."

Danny and Brenda exchanged disgusted looks as Ray downed another gulp and wiped his mouth with his hand.

Brenda walked quickly down the street to Laurie's house. Her sunglasses were in her back pocket, and she wished it weren't dark so that she could wear them. She was beginning to feel self-conscious. What if this didn't work? She had some doubts.

And Ray — Ray was just the kind of guy

Laurie would have a field day with. Give her half a chance and she'd be telling the whole school that Brenda and Ray were engaged to be married — or something else dumb. Danny would just have to keep him away from the house. She'd say what she had come to say and make a swift exit.

When she got to the front of the house she could hear the music coming from inside. The large front yard was lit up and she halted before walking into the bright open space. She turned back when she heard a strange sound coming from the middle of the street. For a second, she wasn't sure what it was. Then she saw Ray running toward her.

"Heeyyy, Woooo, Wooooo," Ray screeched with his arms outstretched. He looked like a giant scarecrow holding up his bottle. Danny was not far behind.

"Cool it, Ray!" commanded Danny.

Ray ignored him and stood in the middle of the street, laughing and doing what looked like some kind of awkward dance.

"Let's go back to Garfield House," ordered Brenda in a no-nonsense voice. Ray was too far out there already for her to risk knocking on the Benningtons' door. Her day with Laurie Bennington would have to wait. She and Danny had to get this jerk back to the halfway house right away.

Brenda and Danny approached Ray from either side and tried to take his hands and lead him back to the car. But Ray avoided them and then raced off toward the bushes near the garage.

He was surprisingly fast. By the time they rounded the corner, Brenda just caught a glimpse of his long arms as he hoisted himself over the Benningtons' fence.

"Oh, no," Brenda moaned.

"What are we going to do?" Danny asked.

"We've got to go in there and get him, but how are we going to get over that fence?"

Ray pointed at what looked like a gate. The two friends ran forward and found it unlocked. When they swung it open, they found themselves in the big backyard which was decorated for Laurie's party. Just ahead, Ray was spinning like a windmill and still swinging his bottle of vodka.

"How did I ever get into this," Brenda wondered out loud.

The huge yard was elaborately landscaped with clusters of small trees, bushes, a rock garden, and a small waterfall. Beyond that was a big swimming pool and a row of swinging Japanese lanterns. Ray was heading toward the water.

Brenda shuddered to think of what would happen if he fell in. Laurie out back scolding and scoffing, telling everyone what a lowlife Brenda was with her sleazy friends. But thankfully, Ray didn't go any closer. He seemed to be slowing down. Finally, he looked around, confused, took another gulp of vodka and sat down on a stone bench.

Danny and Brenda confidently moved forward. Now was their chance to nab him. Nobody was around. Ray couldn't really be seen from the house. With any luck, they'd have him out of the yard, and Laurie would never be the wiser. That's when Brenda heard the voice. It almost made her jump out of her shoes.

"What are you doing here?"

Brenda's stomach clenched. The person who had spoken came forward into the light, and she saw that it was none other than her own step-sister.

"Howdy there, little lady number two," Ray greeted Chris in his mumbling, rambling, drunken way.

Brenda felt her cheeks burn. "Danny, can you please get him out of here," she urged.

Ray had set his bottle on the ground, and Danny sneaked up from behind and snatched it. Without Ray seeing it, he hid the bottle under another bench.

"Hey, where's my bottle?" Ray mumbled finally.

"It's back at the car, Ray." Danny talked to Ray as if he were talking to a five-year-old. "Let's go back to the car, and I'll get you more. Okay?"

Ray looked around vaguely, but gave up with a shrug. He nodded dully and let Danny lead him back through the bushes.

Brenda and Chris stood there alone and listened to Danny and Ray's voices fade away. Chris looked toward the house and was relieved that the music seemed to have covered the commotion in the back yard. As far as she could tell, no one inside had noticed.

Brenda felt humiliated. Her plan had backfired in the worst possible way. She wasn't sure what to do.

"Nice friends you have there," muttered Chris.

She was still in shock over having her solitude invaded and then discovering that it was Brenda.

Brenda put a hand on her hip. "He's not my friend," she said quickly. She let a layer of dark hair cover one side of her face.

"You could have fooled me," Chris answered angrily.

"I mean, one of them is my friend, Danny. But I don't know that creepy guy," Brenda said nervously.

"So what did you do, look for the biggest jerk you could find from the street and bring him here?"

"Funny," Brenda said sarcastically.

"Look, none of you were invited here. You're not wanted. Just go home, okay!"

"What are you trying to say, Chris? That I'm not as good as you and your snooty friends? Is that it?" Brenda felt the edge in her voice and knew that soon there would be no holding back.

Chris flashed another look toward the house. "You said it, not me."

"I bet you never thought I was good enough to join your up tight family."

"Look, it's not my fault that you get in trouble and hang out with creeps like that. It's not my fault if I do well in school and you don't."

Brenda stepped forward. "No, but did you ever think that if you just once, gave me a chance and stopped treating me like I had leprosy or something that I might not be such a terrible person?"

Brenda's voice was strong and angry, but she was surprised to find that she was holding back tears. She and Chris had never confronted each other like this.

"I've given you plenty of chances, and all you do is blow them!" Chris insisted. "Whenever anything goes wrong, you just run back to that halfway house and those awful kids. What do you expect . . ."

"Now, wait a minute," Brenda interrupted. "Okay. That kid who was just there was a creep . . ."

"I'll say he was a creep. . . ."

Brenda continued without waiting for Chris to finish, ". . . but he is not my friend! Most of the kids at the halfway house are really good people! Like Danny. Do you know why Danny went to Garfield House? 'Cause his mom was drunk all the time and he couldn't stand it. It wasn't Danny's fault. And I've got news for you, I bet Danny is smarter, nicer, better than most of your friends."

"Well great, then, why don't you just hang out there all the time and leave me alone? If you think your friends are so fantastic, what are you doing here?" The adrenaline was rushing through Chris's veins and her hands were shaking.

"Oh, just forget it! You've never understood anything about me and you never will. And do you know why?"

"Why?" Chris challenged furiously.

"Because you are so concerned with doing the right thing and never making a mistake that you are totally intolerant of everyone else! You know, I feel sorry for you . . ."

"Oh, you do . . ."

"Yes, I do! How come you're sitting out here all alone? I thought your fabulous friends were supposed to be at this party. Well, if they're such good friends and they like you so much, how come you're sitting out here all by yourself when everybody else is inside having a good time?"

Chris felt like she had been shoved hard in the center of her chest, like someone had just knocked the wind out of her. She was unable to speak.

"Don't worry. I'll leave before your wonderful friend Laurie Bennington finds out. I wouldn't want anybody to think I'd contaminated her backyard or anything. But I'd think about it if I were you, Chris. Maybe my friends aren't student body officers or straight-A students, but they care about me. They would never desert me if I needed them or turn me away if I were in trouble. And that's what matters as far as I'm concerned!"

Brenda's voice rang out across the yard as the music inside suddenly went dead. For a second, there was silence. Both girls stood very still, waiting to see if anyone had heard them. Then, Brenda turned quickly and backed away through the bushes. Chris could hear the light pounding of Brenda's boots as her stepsister reached the gate, then ran off and down the street.

Chris slunk down on the nearest bench. The music started up again, and no one seemed to have heard anything, but she wouldn't have cared if they had. Brenda's words were ringing in her ears. Chris felt like she had just been slapped and her cheeks stung.

Was it true? Was she intolerant? Had Phoebe been right when she'd said Chris didn't know what friendship was? She certainly had alienated Ted and Phoebe, the two people she cared about most. Maybe she *was* too concerned with always behaving the right way and upholding standards. After all, both Phoebe and Ted had come to her when they needed someone, when they were down, and what had she done? Instead of helping and trying to understand, she had only made things worse. And now the damage was done and she had probably lost both of them forever. Brenda was absolutely right. Helping a friend who was in trouble did matter most of all.

Chris no longer wanted to cry. She was beyond that. Leaning over, she rested her elbows on her knees and let her head hang down as if she were dizzy. She wrapped her hands around her calves and rested her forehead on her knee.

Suddenly, she felt something hard and cold against the palm of her hand. She reached under the bench and found a large bottle sitting just behind her leg. As she raised the bottle into the light she saw it was half full. The torn label read VODKA.

Chris looked over toward the house. She could still see the colors dance by the video screen. The wind blew against her face, and she heard a peal of happy laughter ring out from the house. Without making a conscious decision, she lifted the bottle and set it on her lap. She unscrewed the top. After taking a deep breath, she raised the bottle of vodka to her lips and swallowed as much as she could.

Chapter *20*

Phoebe was the first to walk out into the backyard after the videos were over. The other kids were crowding into the kitchen to make their own sundaes, but Phoebe still had no appetite and wanted a breath of fresh air. She closed the sliding glass door, then walked to the edge of the pool where she tested the water with her fingers.

When she first saw Chris emerge from the corner of the yard, she almost turned around to go back inside. But she noticed something strange about Chris that made her stop. She was giggling and swaying in a very un-Chris-like way. Her long blond hair was swinging from side to side, and there was a huge silly smile on her face. Her usually light complexion looked reddish, as if she had been running, and there was a smudge of dirt on her white cords. Even though it was chilly, she had taken off her blue sweater and tied it around her waist. The tails of her white cotton blouse flapped as she wavered from side to side. She moved like some wacky modern dancer as she skipped around the pool and approached her friend.

"Hiya, Phoebe," Chris slurred and threw her arm around Phoebe's neck.

Phoebe pulled back and stared at her best friend. She had never seen Chris act like this. It seemed Chris was drunk, but she just couldn't believe it.

"Hi, Chris. You okay?" Phoebe asked nervously.

"I'm great. I'm wonnnnderful," she sang. "Do you know what?"

"What?" Phoebe answered unsurely.

"You are my very best friend, do you know that? Well, you are, you know. You are one of the bestest people in the whole wide world and I think you're great." Chris started to giggle and gave Phoebe a big hug.

Chris stepped back and lifted the vodka bottle from under a nearby bench. With a grin to Phoebe, she cocked her head back and took a long drink. Phoebe still couldn't believe what she was seeing. Chris Austin was actually drunk!

"Want some?" giggled Chris with a wink. "S'wonderful." Chris started to spin in a circle with her arms outstretched.

Phoebe reached in and easily took the bottle away. "No thanks," she said in an amazed voice. She put the bottle back on the bench.

"Wheeee," squealed Chris as she spun again.

Phoebe was torn between shock, concern, and

amusement. "Take it easy, Chris," she cautioned. Chris responded by putting her finger to her lips and shushing herself.

Phoebe's heart sank as she looked up and saw two people coming out of the kitchen back door and into the far end of the yard. As they came closer, though, she was relieved to see that it was Sasha and Peter. Both he and Sasha were carrying a large dish of ice cream. At once, Chris noticed them too.

"HIIII!" Chris waved cheerily. "It's Sasha and Peter!"

Chris gave them each an emotional hug. Peter and Sasha raised their dishes into the air to avoid getting covered with ice cream.

"You are my friends. If you ever need me, I promise I'll be there if you need . . . oh, you know what I mean," Chris said seriously. When she stepped back from hugging Peter, Chris almost tripped over one of the landscaped rock clusters and started to giggle again. Peter and Sasha stood there openmouthed.

"She's drunk," Phoebe said in a funny voice.

"Obviously," answered Peter.

Phoebe, Peter, and Sasha watched as Chris skipped over to a tree in the corner of the yard and began to sing.

Phoebe took control. "Peter, go get Ted," she ordered. Peter nodded and disappeared into the house. "Sasha, make sure nobody else comes out here for a while, okay?"

Sasha saluted with a short laugh. "I'll do my best."

Phoebe jogged over to the other side of the

pool and found Chris leaning against a tree. She was no longer singing. Chris was looking up to the sky and had her arms wrapped around her chest.

"Phoebe," Chris said sadly.

"What?"

"I'm a terrible friend." Chris tossed her head from side to side. "I'm a terrible, terrible friend."

"No, you're not, Chris," Phoebe soothed.

"Honest?" Chris squeaked in a little-girl voice.

"Honest." Phoebe paused and checked to see if anyone else was coming outside.

"But I should have been more nicer when you were upset. You would never have done that to me, would you?"

"Don't worry about it. We can talk about it later," Phoebe counseled warmly. "Chris, where did you get that liquor?"

Chris slid down the trunk of the tree and plopped onto the ground. She tugged on the sleeves of the sweater tied around her waist and closed her eyes. She opened them very quickly. "Whoa, I'm spinning, Pheeb."

Phoebe sat down next to her. Chris leaned her head lightly on Phoebe's shoulder.

"Chris, do you feel sick?"

"I feel strange," marveled Chris. "Brenda . . ." Her voice trailed off.

"What about Brenda?" asked Phoebe.

"I got the bottle from Brenda. Except it wasn't from Brenda, it was from her friend. Except he wasn't really her friend, the other one was her friend."

"Oh." Phoebe was totally confused.

"See, Brenda was going to crash the party, but her friend was a creep and he left his bottle here . . ."

"I see." Phoebe didn't see at all, but she realized this was not the time to try to figure it out.

Chris leaned forward and pointed her finger. "You know, I never gave Brenda a chance. She's not so bad. She really isn't."

Phoebe looked up to see Ted walking slowly around the pool and onto the small patch of grass where they were sitting. She nudged Chris. "Chris, look who's here."

Chris raised her face and lit up with a delightful glow. "It's Ted!" she said. Her voice was full of wonder and love.

Ted stood there looking down at her with a questioning smile on his face. He started to crouch down next to Chris but was knocked over as she flew at him in a passionate embrace. They both tumbled onto the grass.

"Heyyy," laughed Ted, "we should put you on the football team." He sat up and smoothed the tangled locks of blond hair out of Chris's face. She took his hand and held it against her cheek.

"I love you, Ted Mason," she cried and threw her arms around his neck. For a moment, Ted hesitated and looked at Phoebe, who was leaning back against the tree. Phoebe and Ted smiled at each other. Ted closed his eyes and wrapped Chris in his arms.

They stayed like that until Chris slowly let go and stood up. She was unsteady, but grinning. She took Ted's hands to pull him up too. With gleaming, mischievous eyes, she looked at the swimming pool.

" 'Member what a great time we had when we swam at the Y that time? 'Member we played water volleyball. Let's play water volleyball!" She looked at the water hungrily.

"Chris, there's no volleyball," Ted told her patiently. He was watching her with amusement and great affection.

"Oh." Chris thought for a second. "Well, let's just go for a swim," she said. She kicked off one of her flats and bent down to take off the other.

Ted bent at the waist and talked to Chris with his head upside down. "Chris, we don't have bathing suits," he reminded her.

Chris sprang up. "We don't need any!" She started to untie her sweater from her waist when she fell back on the grass in a heap.

Ted and Phoebe exchanged looks and started to laugh.

"We'd better get this girl home before she does something she really regrets," Ted said to Phoebe.

Chris was still sitting on the grass trying to figure out how to untie her sweater.

Phoebe moved in close to Ted. "Ted, we can't take her home. Her father would kill her. Let's take her to my house. My folks are away. She can sleep over."

"Good idea," agreed Ted. "My car will only hold the two of us. Can you get a ride with Peter or somebody and we'll meet at your house?"

"Sure. I'll go in and get Peter. I'll be right

back. Keep her clothes on," joked Phoebe as she darted into the house.

Chris still sat on the grass, and Ted knelt down next to her. "You are one goofy girl," he said and touched her cheek.

Chris got up on her knees. She had given up on her sweater. She felt dizzy and hot, and wasn't quite sure how she had gotten that way. All she knew was that Ted was next to her and he wasn't mad at her any more. She leaned forward and let her head fall against his chest. He was warm and strong, and the slight scratchiness of his sweater felt good against her forehead. All she wanted was to be as close to him as she could. She let her eyes close as she breathed in his familiar, spicy smell. Suddenly, her head started to spin violently. Her eyes popped back open as she tried to make the sickening motion stop.

Teld held her up with one arm around her back. Kissing her on the brow, he stroked the back of her head with his other hand.

Chris was starting to feel ill. She was very hot. Her head felt like it was turning around and around and her stomach was queasy. It was like riding on a tiny boat in the middle of the most violent storm. Chris knew that she was on solid ground, but everything around her was lurching. She collapsed against Ted and released a tiny moan.

"Uh, oh," caressed Ted. "Poor baby. I have a feeling this is going to be a long night." He wiped her forehead with the cuff of his sweater and hugged her closer.

Peter quickly followed Phoebe into the backyard. He pulled on his denim jacket and searched his pockets for his car keys.

Phoebe was relieved to see that Chris and Ted were in the shadows and so far no one outside of close friends had seen them. She hoped they would be able to get Chris to her house without much trouble. Phoebe's pulse picked up when she heard the glass door glide open and shut with an angry thump. Peter continued to look for his keys and didn't notice anything until he heard the voice.

"Peter, you aren't leaving, are you?"

It was Laurie. She was walking directly over to where they all were. Ted's head popped up nervously. Laurie walked right up to them. "What's going on?" she asked in an irritated tone.

Phoebe jumped right in. "Chris doesn't feel very well, so we're going to take her home."

Ted and Peter were silent, but Chris let out a slight moan.

"What's wrong with her?" Laurie snapped.

"Stomach ache," blurted Phoebe. She was shocked by Laurie's nasty tone and knew she was right to try to hide Chris's indiscretion. But Phoebe turned her head and the first thing that caught her eye was the bottle of vodka on the bench behind her. She tried to pretend she wasn't looking at anything, but it was too late. Laurie followed her gaze and spotted the bottle, too. Just at that moment, Chris began to sing.

Angrily, Laurie walked over and picked up the bottle. "A stomach ache?" she said sarcastically. "What kind of a party does she think this is? Gross. She's as bad as her sister."

Ted flinched. He and Phoebe looked at each other. Finally, Laurie Bennington was showing her true colors, and they were not very pretty.

Ted helped lift Chris to her feet and started to walk her toward the side gate. Peter followed.

"Peter," Laurie called, "Ted can take her home. Where are you going?"

Peter stopped and replied without turning around to face Laurie. "He needs help."

"Well, then you're coming back, right?" She came up close to him and spoke in a soft voice. "Remember my father. He won't be here until late and he really wants to meet you. And we can have some time alone together."

Peter turned around briskly. "Look, Laurie, thanks for trying to introduce me to your father and all, but Ted needs help with Chris." He looked right at her.

Laurie slowly lifted her hand and touched Peter's cheek, then her expression changed. "Oh, all right. Go ahead and help your drunken Goldilocks. But just remember to come back right away."

Peter took Laurie's hand and removed it from his face. Finally, he was in control. He had had enough of Laurie Bennington's manipulation. "Thanks for the party, Laur. See you in school next week."

"Do you mean you're really leaving and you're not coming back?" Laurie looked like she was about to start screaming.

Peter smiled slightly. "You got it. Great party, Laur. G'night." He waved and walked straight out the side gate and into the street.

Laurie watched Chris and Ted, Phoebe and Peter. She was steaming as she saw them march out of the yard and down the street. Her hands were balled up in little fists with her long nails digging into her palms. Short little puffs of air huffed out of her nose. Laurie was furious. Peter had rejected her after all her planning and effort, and it was all Chris's fault. Chris Austin had spoiled her party! Laurie was going to have to find some way to pay her back.

"You aren't getting away with this, Austin!" Laurie cried. "Do you hear me? Do you hear me, Chris?"

Eyes closed, her head lolling back against the passenger seat of Ted's MG, Chris didn't hear a thing.

Chapter
21

"Hurry up, Phoebe!" Ted prayed to himself as he sat on the Halls' front doorstep and held Chris in his arms. By now, Chris was breathing in long gulps and obviously trying to ease the waves of nausea that were convulsing her insides.

Chris had never felt so sick in her life. She was thankful Ted was holding her, and she clung to him with all her remaining strength, but she still felt out of control. Her insides were rocking and swaying, and the spinning was getting worse. If this was what it was like to get drunk, she had no desire ever to do it again. Every so often, she would hear a slow, pathetic moan and realize a moment later that the sound was coming out of her own throat!

"It's okay now, Chris, we're out of the car," comforted Ted. He rubbed the back of Chris's neck lightly.

"Uh huh," moaned Chris. She sat up a little

straighter and was relieved to find that her sickness eased a bit in that position. Feeling a touch stronger, Chris anchored her hands on Ted's shoulders and slowly stood up. Ted had tied her sweater over her shoulders, but she still felt hot so she slipped the knotted sleeves over her head, causing the sweater to sail onto the ground. She let go of Ted's shoulders and found she was able to balance on her own.

"How you doin'?" Ted asked with concern.

"Mmmmmm. Better. Much better," nodded Chris as she half stumbled down the steps and into the circular driveway. "I think I'm going to be okay," she vowed with a wave of her hand.

Ted watched closely as Chris walked the edge of the driveway as if she were balancing on a tightrope. He had to laugh as she started to sing again in a playful, off-key voice. She was singing the school song. At the climactic finish, she let her voice ring out and spread her arms like an Olympic gymnast finishing a routine. With a giggle, she twirled awkwardly around with her arms spread wide.

"Yaaaayyyy!" she sang gaily as she continued to reel and whirl. She finally stopped and caught her breath. With a slight waver, she walked back over to Ted.

"Pretty good, Austin," he applauded.

Chris clapped, too, and spun around, then sat next to Ted on the front steps.

Without any warning, Chris's happy recovery halted. She sat up very still for a split second before pitching her upper body towards the edge of the steps. She knew she was going to be violently ill. With a wrenching spasm, her stomach announced that it had had enough.

Phoebe and Peter pulled up in his Volkswagon in time to see Chris bent over the edge of the steps, Ted rubbing her back and trying to soothe her obvious pain.

"Oh, no," sympathized Peter as he ran up the driveway.

Phoebe quickly pulled out her house keys. "Ted, can you get her to my room?"

Ted stretched his arms a bit, as if getting ready for an important play in a football game. "Chris, I'm going to carry you inside. Can you make it to Phoebe's room?"

Chris raised her head and nodded miserably. Ted easily lifted her. As soon as Phoebe unlocked the front door, he carried her down the hall and gracefully laid her down in Phoebe's bedroom.

Chris sprawled on the bed. Although the worst of her sickness was over, she didn't feel any better. Now her throat was burning and her head felt dry and hollow. She was still unsure of where she was or how she had gotten there. She felt something wet and cool on her forehead and realized that Ted was wiping her face with a damp cloth.

"How's that?" he whispered.

"Nice," Chris answered weakly. She felt like she was about to cry, but she didn't have the energy. Shifting herself slightly on the bed, she rested her head on Ted's lap. She looked up at him. "I'm sorry."

Ted smiled and wiped the nape of her neck with the wet washcloth. "I'm sorry, too," he said.

Ted came slowly downstairs and found Phoebe in the kitchen talking on the telephone. She signaled for him to be silent as she continued her conversation.

"Do you want to talk to her, Mrs. Austin? But she just went upstairs to pull out the cot. I'll tell her anything you need her to know." Phoebe paused and looked at Ted. "Oh, don't worry, she can wear my nightgown, and I even have an extra toothbrush for her. It's no trouble." She looked again at Ted and crossed her fingers. "Thanks, Mrs. Austin. Talk to you tomorrow." Phoebe hung up.

"Phew," she said to Ted.

"Did you pull it off?" Ted asked.

"I don't think Catherine or her father suspect anything. How's Chris doing?"

Ted pushed up the sleeves of his sweater and sat down at the kitchen table. "She's asleep."

Phoebe leaned against the counter. "Peter went home. He cleaned up out front first. I think that was friendship above and beyond the call of duty." She laughed softly and opened the overhead cabinet.

"I'd say the same thing goes for you," Ted added. "Thanks."

Phoebe shrugged. "Want something? I'm having some tea."

"Okay. After what Chris has been through, I think that's about the only thing I could swallow."

It was quiet, and both Phoebe and Ted were slowing down after the crisis of the last hour. It was dark in the street, and the front porch light shone in through the kitchen window. A light wind whistled and fluttered the curtains. Phoebe could feel the energy fading from her muscles, leaving them sore and tired. She and Ted sat quietly and drank their tea.

"You really love Chris, don't you?" Phoebe asked finally, breaking the silence.

Ted looked off and smiled. "Yeah. I didn't even realize how much until these last two weeks. It's funny. Chris and I are really different people, you know. But I think that's what's good about us being together. That we're different. It's dumb to get so upset just because the other person does something you don't think is cool, or whatever. I mean, just because two people are a couple it doesn't mean they're the same person, right?" Ted put his cup down. "Geez, am I even making sense?"

Phoebe sat down next to him and leaned on the table. "Sure," she said.

"I don't care about what people think or how you're supposed to act. I know Chris is hung up about that kind of stuff and that's okay with me. Probably, it's good for me to have somebody around who worries like that. Keeps me in line."

"Well, she can hardly stand up as a perfect example after tonight," Phoebe smiled.

"Yeah." Ted laughed. "That's good, too. I don't know. The important thing is how you feel about each other, isn't it?"

Phoebe paused. She thought about Griffin. *Was* how you felt about each other the most important thing? She didn't answer Ted.

Ted slapped his hands against his thighs and pushed back his chair. "Well, Pheeb, I'm going to go on home. Do you promise to call me if there're any problems?"

"I promise," Phoebe assured him. "Don't worry. I'll take care of her."

Ted wandered to the front door. He opened it and looked out into the yard. "What a night," he exclaimed and tugged down the sleeves of his sweater. With great affection, Ted tousled Phoebe's hair and trotted down the front steps. "Remember, call me if she gets sick again or anything," he said as he walked backward toward his sports car.

"She'll be fine. Don't worry."

"Yeah. Right. G'night." Ted ran his hand through his curly light hair and got into his MG.

Phoebe watched Ted's car disappear around the corner before going back inside. She tiptoed into her bedroom and found Chris sound asleep, breathing heavily. Gently, Phoebe slid her quilt from under Chris's feet and spread it over her.

Phoebe heard what she thought was knocking and slowly walked back to the front hall. As she got closer, she heard the knocking more clearly and wondered if Ted had forgotten something. Smiling to herself, she thought he had probably decided to turn around and come back, too worried about Chris to go on home.

Ready to tease Ted for his overprotectiveness,

Phoebe swung open the door with a mischievous look in her eye. But as soon as she saw who was on the front step, the playful expression left her face, and she felt her insides tighten.

Brad was back from Princeton.

Chapter
22

Brad smiled wearily. In his gray slacks and wrinkled white shirt, he looked like a young executive at the end of a long day. His striped tie was undone and hung around his neck like a limp ribbon. It was obvious that he had started the day looking perfectly pressed and neat — but step by step, the jacket had come off, the sleeves had been rolled up, the tie had been loosened, until he had become the wilted Ivy Leaguer Phoebe saw standing before her.

"Come in," Phoebe said automatically. Her mind was racing. Just seeing Brad's wholesome face again was jarring. He was a different person to her now. So many things had changed since he had gone away a day and a half ago.

Brad came into the entry hall and leaned toward Phoebe to give her a kiss. The gesture was nothing special; it was the normal way they had greeted each other since they had started going together two years ago. But this time Phoebe turned her cheek and backed away into the living room. It was subtle, Phoebe's slipping away before Brad could kiss her, and even he wasn't sure if the slight had been intentional.

Phoebe slid off her shoes and sat cross-legged in her father's large antique rocking chair. It was the one place where Brad would be unable to sit next to her. She tried hard to relax as she rocked slowly. Brad pushed a pile of mismatched pillows aside and plopped down on the couch. The house was very quiet.

"I just got back," Brad volunteered as he rubbed the back of his neck. "The train was kind of late. I went over to Laurie's, but Sasha told me you'd gone home. The party was pretty much breaking up anyway."

Phoebe folded her hands in her lap and looked at Brad. She wondered if he felt the same tension in the air as she did. She wondered if he could tell something about her was different.

"Did Sasha tell you about Chris?"

"She said something about you taking her home because she didn't feel well, something like that."

Good old Sasha, thought Phoebe. Protecting Chris to the end. "Chris had a bad night. She got drunk. She's asleep in my bedroom."

Phoebe almost asked Brad not to spread it around, but she knew he wouldn't do anything to hurt Chris. Brad wouldn't do anything to hurt anybody, she thought guiltily.

"Chris got drunk? That's pretty amazing. Is she okay? Does Ted know?" Brad's square face was a blend of concern and surprise.

Phoebe kept rocking. "Yeah. She got sick, but I think she'll be okay tomorrow. Ted brought her over here. I think they might be starting to get back together."

"Well, that's good. It was really dumb of them to break up in the first place."

Brad slid down to the edge of the couch which was nearest to Phoebe. He took off his polished wingtips and stretched his legs out on the corner of her rocker.

Phoebe sat still. "Well? How was your interview? How did it go?" She had meant for her voice to sound excited, but she knew her questions had come out dull and flat.

Brad smiled and raised his hands. "Who knows. It felt good. I mean, I had answers to all their questions about why I wanted to go there, what I wanted to do, what I thought was important — you know, all that. At first, I was kind of nervous, but I think I did pretty well."

"I'm sure you'll get in," Phoebe said. She gave her hands a quick shake as she realized that her palms were damp and her fingers clenched. She looked up at Brad and smiled sadly.

"I tried to call you this afternoon, but nobody was home."

"Oh. That must have been when I was over at Chris's."

"Yeah," agreed Brad. He suddenly felt uncomfortable and he wasn't sure why. There was an awkward moment of silence. "So. How did your Follies go? Are you a star?" he joked with a forced laugh.

Phoebe sat frozen in her chair. At some point

in the last few minutes, she had made her decision. She knew it was time. She had to tell Brad what had happened with Griffin, but it was almost as if she had forgotten how to speak, as if the sound didn't know how to get out. She stared at her crossed legs. The air around her felt thick and heavy, as if it were holding her in, trapping her, and it would take a great effort to break through.

Removing his feet from Phoebe's chair, Brad sat forward and leaned his elbows on his knees. He scratched the slight stubble on his chin and looked at Phoebe with confusion.

"Uh, did you get the note I dropped off at the theater?" he asked uneasily. He couldn't figure out why Phoebe was acting so strangely.

Phoebe nodded. "Thanks. For the flower, too."

There was a pressure in the back of her throat and Phoebe took a deep breath to keep the tears from coming. This was one time when she did not want to cry. She had to be strong.

"Uh, so, were you good? I mean, did everybody clap a lot, or whatever you wanted them to do?"

Phoebe was silent and couldn't look at him. Finally, drawing on all her courage, she raised her head. With a sweep of her hand she pushed a few wisps of red hair away from her face and looked Brad clearly in the eye. "Brad," she began slowly, "something's happened."

The tone of Phoebe's voice was so odd, so full of doom, that Brad sat up with a start. This is how it is when you find out that someone you know has died, he thought. Whereas a moment ago he had been exhausted, now he felt a surge of panic.

"What, Pheeb. What is it?" he replied slowly.

Still the words were difficult to get out. Phoebe knew that once she had said them, there would be no taking them back, no pretending that her night with Griffin hadn't happened. This was it. She lifted her head high, but she was unable to continue looking Brad in the face. She stared at a spot directly behind his head.

"I've fallen in love with someone else."

The words dropped like a bomb. Brad was totally unprepared and for an instant, he wondered if he had heard her correctly. No, no one had died, but what Phoebe was saying to him was somehow even worse. He couldn't quite grasp it, and it took a while for him to respond at all.

"Who?" Brad finally managed. There was no hostility in his question, just confusion and shock.

Phoebe swallowed hard. "I don't think you know him. His name is Griffin Neill. He was in the Follies."

"Griffin Neill?" Brad looked around jumpily. "Who's he?" It was amazing to Brad that there was someone at Kennedy he didn't know.

"He's a senior. He doesn't hang out with any crowd."

"Wait a minute," Brad said as he stood up. He started pacing to the other side of the cluttered living room. "I don't get it. When did this happen?" He was still so shocked that he was unable to digest it all.

Phoebe spoke calmly. "It started even before

I realized it. I guess when we were rehearsing together. When you were gone, I went out with him."

Brad turned swiftly around. He was beginning to understand. "Do you mean that you've had feelings for this guy, this — what's his name — Griffin, these last two weeks?" He looked at her with a betrayed, painful stare.

"I guess so," Phoebe answered guiltily.

"I don't believe this. I mean, I don't even know how to react. I just . . ." His voice trailed off in disbelief.

Phoebe felt horrible. The last thing she wanted to do was hurt Brad this way. "Oh, Brad, I'm so sorry."

Brad sat down on the couch again. He rested his head in his hands and was quiet for a moment.

"So what about us?" he said finally.

Phoebe wrapped her arms around her chest. "I think we should break up," she said. Her voice was halting and thin, but she had said it.

Brad's head jerked up, and his eyes were clouded with pain. "But, it's okay. I mean, I'll forgive you, Pheeb. We don't have to break up, honest. Just stop seeing this guy and it will all be over."

Phoebe couldn't bear to see Brad so desperate. But she knew she had to hold fast.

"No. I don't want to stop seeing him. And it's dishonest to keep seeing you when I'm in love with somebody else."

"But this thing happened so fast. Maybe you won't feel the same way about him in another week or so. Why don't we just wait and see what happens?" He stopped and rubbed his forehead. "Don't you love me anymore?" he asked in a weak voice.

Phoebe allowed two trickles to wash down her cheeks before willing herself to keep control. She felt guilty and torn. "I still care a lot about you. But I guess I'm not in love with you anymore."

Brad shook his head. Tears were starting to flow from his eyes, too. Angrily he wiped them away. "Oh, Phoebe," he pleaded, "why? I just don't get it. What did I do?"

Leaning forward, Phoebe touched his hand. "It's not your fault. It's me. I guess I'm just not the right person for you, after all."

"But I don't think that," he cried. His voice was getting strained and uneven. "Was it because of the Follies, because I didn't want you to be in them? Was that it?"

"No," Phoebe insisted. "It wasn't anything. I guess I'm just changing."

"So what about this other guy? Is he so much more right for you now than I am?"

"I don't know," Phoebe said harshly. She wanted this painful discussion to end. "All I know is how I feel. Oh, Brad. I don't want to hurt. You're a wonderful person. You'll find somebody else who's much better for you than I am. I wish I could explain it better, but I can't. I'm becoming a different kind of person, that's all I know. I'm so sorry."

Brad sat back. "Are you sure? What if it doesn't work out with this guy?"

"I'm sure," Phoebe answered sadly. "Even if I never see Griffin again, I think it's better for the two of us to split up."

Brad sat very still for a moment before nodding his head in an angry gesture. Quickly, he pulled on his shoes, his hands so tense that he had trouble tying the laces. Without a word, he stood up and went for the front door.

Phoebe jumped up and stood between Brad and the doorway. "Brad." She put her hand on his arm. He angrily pulled his arm away as if he could no longer stand her touching him. Phoebe continued to block his exit. "Can we still be friends? Please?"

Brad didn't answer. He stood with his hands on his hips and looked angrily to one side of her.

"I know you're angry, but we've been together for a long time. We've shared a lot. I still care so much about you. Please, can we still be friends?" Phoebe was practically begging.

Brad finally looked at her. She had never seen such anger, such hatred in his eyes and it cut right through her.

"I don't think so," he spat out. "In fact, I don't think I ever want to talk to you again." He pushed past her and stormed out into the front yard. By the time Phoebe was able to raise her head again, he was gone.

Chapter
23

It was very cold for a fall morning. Phoebe sat alone on her front steps. Frost clung to the grass, although she knew that it would shortly turn to dew. There was just a hint of light on the horizon, and Phoebe found herself hoping with all her heart that the sun would come up again. Of course, she knew it would come up, but she had never stayed awake all night to wait for it before.

Phoebe shivered slightly in the morning chill. She still wore the pink overalls she had worn to the party, and she had wrapped herself in the colorful wool blanket her mother had brought back from Ireland. On her feet was a silly pair of rabbit slippers. Usually, the yellow furry rabbits made her laugh. This morning they simply kept her company.

For a couple of hours she had tried to sleep on

the couch, but she kept flinching and waking up. Then she would go over it all again in her mind. The accusing, betrayed look in Brad's eye kept coming back to her. Every time she thought about him, her heart would begin to pound, and she would shift uncomfortably or sit up with a start.

Now, there was nothing to do but wait for the day to begin all over again. Just seeing the sun peek up in the corner of the sky gave Phoebe hope. But now it was coming back, and soon the sky would be as bright and sunny as ever. Phoebe would just have to do the same thing with her own life.

She wandered inside to check on Chris. When she got to her bedroom, she found her friend tossing and turning. Chris was moaning slightly and trying to cover her head with the pillow. Phoebe tiptoed in and crouched by the bed.

Chris opened her eyes and leaned up on her elbows. She looked around with confusion and then held her head in obvious pain. Seeing Phoebe, her face grew even more puzzled.

"It's okay, Chris," Phoebe comforted softly. "You're at my house."

"I am?" Chris answered with disbelief. Then she let out a long moan and lowered herself down to the pillow. "Why am I at your house?" she asked weakly. Her face was scrunched up as if trying to keep out the tiniest ray of light.

"Don't you remember last night?" Phoebe asked patiently.

"Huh?" A long lock of hair had fallen over Chris's eyes, but she made no attempt to brush it away. "I don't feel good," she said slowly, like a little girl.

Phoebe had to smile. "I bet you don't."

"My head. My head feels terrible. What am I doing here?" Chris dragged herself up to a sitting position and put her palms over her eyes. "I'm thirsty," she added, licking her dry lips.

Phoebe padded into the kitchen and fetched a glass of cold orange juice. The gray light was just starting to filter in the big window over the sink. Just as she closed the refrigerator, Phoebe heard the whack of the Sunday paper being thrown against the front door.

When Phoebe got back to her bedroom, Chris was sitting on the edge of the bed. She was still wearing her white pants and the shirttails of her striped blouse hung sloppily over her hips.

"Here." Phoebe handed her the juice.

"Mmmmmm. Thanks," Chris mumbled, drinking it greedily. Her eyes opened a touch wider, and she looked down at her shirt. "Did I sleep in my clothes? Yuck." She wrinkled her nose and started rubbing her temples again.

Phoebe sat down next to Chris on the bed. "Chris, do you remember Laurie's party last night?"

Chris squinted for a moment and scratched her head. "I think so," she said unsurely. "I remember getting dressed to go and walking over there. And being in the back yard . . ." Chris looked off in confusion. "Oh, Phoebe, are you still mad at me?" she said suddenly. "I remember you were so mad at me. Everybody was mad at me because I was such a terrible friend."

Phoebe smiled. "I'm not mad at you any more."

"Oh, good." Chris sighed. She leaned her head on Phoebe's shoulder. "I sure don't feel very good. My head feels like somebody used it for a bowling ball."

Chris closed her eyes and seemed to be trying to remember something. A second later, her eyes opened wide and she sat up in surprise. "Brenda!" she said.

"What about Brenda?" Phoebe encouraged.

Chris stood up very suddenly. As soon as she did, she let out a sharp moan and held her head again. "Ouwww!" Chris fell back down onto the bed.

Phoebe rubbed Chris's back lightly. "Want more juice?"

Chris nodded carefully and stood up again, this time much more slowly. She followed Phoebe into the kitchen as if she were in slow motion. All she knew was if she moved her head suddenly, it felt like someone was whacking her with a block of wood. Very evenly, she sat down at the kitchen table and waited for another glass of juice.

"Thanks, Pheeb."

Chris swallowed the juice like someone about to die of thirst and set the glass in front of her. For a minute she stared at the empty glass. Suddenly, her mouth fell open. "Oh, no," she said at last.

"What is it, Chris?" Phoebe prodded.

Chris continued staring at the glass. "I remember now," she said flatly. "Ohh. It's all coming back to me."

246

Chris was looking even sicker.

"It started with Brenda. She was in the back-yard and we had a fight. I'm not sure why she was there at Laurie's party, but she was. And she said things to me that really hurt. They really hurt because some of them were true. And there was this jerky kid there at first, before Brenda and I had the fight. He must have been the one who left the bottle behind. I remember how that stuff burned my throat so badly when I drank it and how I started to feel warm all over and kind of happy and . . ." Chris's voice trailed off.

"And?"

"That's all." Chris leaned forward on the table. "Ted," she smiled. "I remember Ted hold-ing me." Her smile faded. "Or maybe I just dreamed that part."

"No." Phoebe told Chris how Ted had brought her over and put her to bed. Chris listened in-tently, and her eyes began to fill with tears.

"I really love him," Chris heaved a sigh.

"I know." Phoebe smiled. "And he knows, too." Phoebe gave Chris a pat and started to look into the overhead cabinet. "Will you eat something? I bet it will make you feel better."

"I'll try." She paused. "Phoebe, what did I do at Laurie's party?"

Phoebe melted some butter in a frying pan and pulled out a carton of eggs and a loaf of bread. "Oh, you danced on the table top and kissed all the boys and put a lampshade on your head."

"I did?" Chris looked mortified.

Phoebe laughed. "Not really. Mainly, you told

your friends how much you liked them. It was kind of nice. You did ask Ted to skinny dip in the pool, though." She broke a few eggs in a bowl, scrambled them and poured them into the pan.

Chris blushed deep red. "You're kidding. Did everybody know I was drunk?"

"Don't worry, just your closest friends. I don't think any of them will spread it around." Phoebe wondered if Laurie would be so kind. Now that Laurie had shown herself to be so nasty, Phoebe wouldn't want to trust her with anything. She decided not to worry Chris about it.

Chris got up and refilled her glass with cold water. "I must have been pretty disgusting."

Phoebe turned and touched Chris's hand. "No, just human. We all make mistakes."

Chris felt her shoulders begin to shake first. By the time she turned to hug Phoebe, the tears were rolling silently down her cheeks. Phoebe hugged her back.

"Hey, you were a little bit disgusting when you came back here and threw up in the bushes. I'm not letting you off that easily," Phoebe joked.

Chris was laughing and crying at the same time. "Oh, Phoebe," she cried, "I'm sorry I wasn't there for you when you needed me. I'm sorry I didn't understand." Chris sat back at the table alternately sniffing and giggling as Phoebe turned away to put some bread in the toaster. "I'm sorry I didn't take your feelings for Griffin more seriously. You came to me for help, and I didn't even listen to you. I'm sorry."

Phoebe set two plates on the table and scraped

the eggs from the pan. "Apology accepted. It doesn't matter anymore. It's all over now." Phoebe ate hungrily while Chris moved her food around with her fork, taking only an occasional bite.

"What do you mean, it's over?" Chris asked.

Phoebe stopped eating. "I broke up with Brad last night after he got back from Princeton."

Chris put her fork down and looked up. "You did? Are you okay?"

"Yes. I know I did the right thing. It was awful, really awful. But I'm so in love with Griffin that I just had to. It would be a joke to pretend I didn't care for him."

Phoebe pictured Griffin's sensitive face and started to feel warm all over. "When Griffin told me he loved me, more than anything, I wanted to tell him I loved him back. Because I do. But Brad was standing between us. I mean, Griffin was able to give himself to me, totally, but I wasn't. That's what I want to do now. Love somebody totally. That's what life's really all about. I want to tell Griffin how I feel." Phoebe was amazed at the strength of her own voice. She looked over at Chris and saw that her friend was starting to cry again.

It was a strange kind of sadness that Chris felt. She wasn't sobbing or weeping, she was almost smiling, but the tears kept sliding down her cheeks. It felt good to cry. "If you truly love Griffin, you have to tell him, you have to let him know. Don't wait."

There was something in Chris's voice that made Phoebe stop eating and look up at her friend. It was a tone, a catch, a depth Phoebe had rarely heard before from anyone.

"Why do you say that?" she asked softly.

More tears spilled down Chris's beautiful cheeks. With a short laugh, she blew her nose on a paper napkin and took a deep breath. "I've never told anyone this," Chris began, "but when my mom was, you know, in the hospital for the last time . . ."

"Yes," Phoebe encouraged.

"Well, the last couple of weeks, she was so sick she wasn't really like my mom anymore. I mean, she looked so different, so thin and pale, and you couldn't tell if she could hear you or not. My dad would be there all the time in the room with her. He kept telling everyone how strong I was and how proud he was of me and all. Anyway, right at the end, I wanted to tell my mom that I loved her, but I knew if I did I would totally fall apart and she probably couldn't hear me anyway. So I didn't. I didn't tell her . . ."

Chris's voice faltered. She wiped her tears with the back of her hand. "But later, I realized that she probably would have heard me, somehow, you know, and 'I love you' should have been the last thing I said to her. And then she died and it was over. It was too late."

"Chris, I'm sure she knew . . ."

"I know," Chris said with one sharp, final sniff. "I just mean that you should let the people you care about know how you feel. And you shouldn't wait because, I don't know, they may not always be there. Right?"

Phoebe looked at Chris's watery blue eyes, so

full of pain, and of love. "Right."

"And I guess it's more important to love people and let them know than to worry about being strong or doing what you think you're supposed to do. Right?"

"Right." Phoebe laughed.

Chris began to laugh softly, too. She and Phoebe looked at each other, breaking into huge, happy smiles. Suddenly, they both felt very strong and alive.

When Ted called an hour later, he and Chris made a date to ride to school together on Monday and start to patch things up. By the time the sun was fully risen, Phoebe and Chris were lounging in the living room finishing off a box of coffee cake. Chris was in the middle of a bite when she turned over on the couch and drifted off. A moment later, Phoebe climbed out of her father's rocker, grabbed a pillow, and curled up on the floor. They both slept peacefully until late in the afternoon.

Chapter 24

When Chris woke up, it was three-fifteen and she felt like she might actually recover. There was still a dull ache in the back of her head, but it was nothing compared to the way she had felt that morning. After showering and washing her hair, she felt downright human.

Since Phoebe was not allowed to drive her father's Audi, and her parents had not yet returned from the mountains, Chris called Catherine and asked if she would pick her up. Catherine agreed cheerfully, seeming to suspect nothing of the last night's misadventures.

Chris sat in the living room combing out her wet hair as she waited for her stepmother. She wore a purple sweatshirt of Phoebe's and had managed to wash the dirt smudges out of her pants. Her skin was tinged with a healthy pink, and her eyes were clear and lively.

"Phoebe," Chris said.

Phoebe was filing her nails and her hair was wrapped in a big blue towel. She also looked well rested and calm. "Hmmmmm?"

"Thanks. You're a true friend."

Phoebe smiled. "So are you, Austin."

The girls came together for a short hug when the doorbell rang with an insistent buzz.

Chris gathered up her sweater and blouse and ran to open the door and greet her stepmother.

"Hi," said the figure in the doorway. She looked down with embarrassment. "I'm here to drive you home," she added.

Chris felt a slight skip in her heartbeat. Standing before her was Brenda, wearing black Levis and a funky striped blazer. Chris blushed and finished her good bye to Phoebe. There was an awkward silence as she and Brenda walked out to the car and climbed into the front seat.

Brenda started to say something but hesitated and remained silent. She reached forward to start the engine, but Chris stopped her.

"Wait," Chris said nervously. "I want to tell you something." This time, she wanted to get things straight right away.

Brenda turned and faced her. Her dark glasses were holding her hairback like a headband, but she made no attempt to pull them down. She looked at Chris openly, without hostility.

"I want you to know that I got very drunk last night after you left Laurie's party. What you said really upset me" — Chris hesitated — "because I guess it's partly true . . . anyway, I picked up the bottle that kid left and I got drunk."

Brenda's mouth fell open. Her eyes registered

pure shock. At last, she broke into a full, free smile, one of the first Chris had ever seen on her face. "You drank that awful vodka that guy left? I bet you got really sick."

"Don't remind me," Chris replied.

Brenda started to laugh, but then put her hand over her mouth.

"You can laugh, it's okay." Chris began to laugh too.

"I guess I just can't imagine you drunk," Brenda smiled shyly.

"Yeah, well. We all make mistakes."

Brenda looked at Chris with the most amazed, fawnlike eyes, but then, too embarrassed to respond, she started the engine. Just before releasing the brake, she turned to Chris. "I was pretty hard on you last night," she said hurriedly. "I'm sorry."

Brenda seemed about to say something else but she cleared her throat instead.

Chris wanted to make sure Brenda knew her outlook had changed. "There's been a lot of misunderstanding between you and me. What do you say we give it another chance and try to be friends? I mean, we're already sisters."

Brenda gripped the steering wheel. Slowly, she relaxed her hands and turned to Chris. "Okay. Let's give it a try," she said awkwardly. She pulled the car into the street.

There was no further conversation on the way home, but it didn't matter. Chris knew it would take a lot before she and Brenda really understood each other. But at least the first step had been taken.

Late that night Phoebe sat up in her bed and tried to read. She didn't feel the least bit tired. Having slept most of the afternoon, she now felt fresh and energetic. She wondered how she would ever fall asleep and get enough rest for school tomorrow. It was strange even to think about school, about going back to the routine of history and gym and computer math. This weekend had changed her whole world, and she wasn't sure that anything would look the same on Monday.

Phoebe couldn't wait to see Griffin again. She still felt anxious and awful when she thought about Brad and how she had hurt him, but she knew she had done the right thing.

She hoped that one day Brad would forgive her and they would be able to be friends again. Phoebe was beginning to understand that even if Griffin had not come along, it would have ended between her and Brad. It had been over for a lot longer than she had realized. Brad was steady and good, hardworking and kind. But he didn't care about the things in the world that meant the most to her. He was too set on his one-way path to Princeton and medical school to think much about feelings, or experience a new way of looking at the world. Phoebe realized that some of the problems in their relationship had been her fault. She had allowed herself almost to become Brad's secretary, like her mom was to her dad. That soda pop feeling had been a sign telling her she was holding her real self down. Phoebe knew she still had a lot to learn — she

255

wasn't sure what it was she wanted to do with her life. But she felt like she was finally on the road to finding out.

Phoebe opened her shutters and got up on her knees. It was very dark, but the sky was clear and the stars bright. She slid open her window to let in the fresh, cold air and wrapped her quilt around her shoulders.

She could hear the television faintly from the living room. Her father was talking back to the news announcer. Her mother was on the phone in the kitchen and every so often, her musical laugh would float down the hall. Phoebe was glad that the house was full again.

With a strong push, she slid her window all the way up and stuck her head out. The air was refreshing, and she could smell the damp earth of the flower bed just below her. She was just ducking back inside when she heard a tiny pinging sound echo against the side of the house.

Phoebe stuck her head out as far as she could. Half kneeling on her bed, she held onto the window frame for support. She thought she heard a whispery sound. For a second, she almost imagined she heard someone calling her name. But then, the sound stopped. Silence. Another ping against the side of the house.

"Hello? Is someone out there?" Phoebe asked tentatively. She was a little scared. It was too dark to see much of anything, but she thought she saw movement near the big oak tree.

"Phoebe? Phoebe, is that you?"

Phoebe recognized the voice at once. Her entire body felt a rush of excitement. There was no way to contain the smile that burst onto her face.

"Griffin!"

Then she saw him. He followed her voice and appeared out of the darkness. In the glow of the front porch light, Phoebe could see his short, dark jacket. A light wool scarf was draped around his neck.

Griffin stepped into the flower bed and rose on his toes to hug Phoebe through the window. His skin was so warm and soft — Phoebe closed her eyes and took in every sensation. She relaxed her loving hold on him, but Griffin continued to hold her tighter and tighter until it almost hurt.

Griffin spoke quickly as if he were rushing somewhere. "I just looked up your address, but when I got here I couldn't figure out which window was yours. I thought if I threw stones you'd know it was me."

Phoebe smiled and brushed back Griffin's silky hair. "Why didn't you just go to the front door like a normal person?"

Griffin looked at her as if it had never occured to him to go to the front door. "I don't know. I figured it was too late and I guess I didn't want to deal with your parents."

"I can't figure you out, Neill," Phoebe sighed happily. She stacked her pillows up and used them as a step to lift herself up. Grabbing the frame of the window, Phoebe squeezed herself awkwardly through until she dropped onto the ground next to him.

Immediately he pulled her into his arms, and she could feel the fierceness of his grip through her long flannel nightgown. Again he held her tightly. There was something in his embrace that Phoebe didn't understand. He hugged her as if he would never see her again.

"You look so beautiful," he whispered.

An easy wind came up, making Phoebe's hair even fuller and curlier. She let it cover her face and clung to Griffin. He continued to hold her with a strange desperation. "What is it, Griffin? Is something wrong?"

At last Griffin relaxed his arms and looked longingly at her face. He took her hands. "No. Yes . . . I don't know," was all he could say.

"What is it? Tell me."

Griffin continued to hold her hands but looked down at the ground as if he were trying to figure something out. At last he raised his head. "Woody's parents brought a friend of theirs to see the Follies. This friend is an agent in New York, and he called me this morning. He wants me to come to New York and audition for a new Broadway play."

Phoebe threw her arms around him. "Griffin, that's wonderful! That's great! I knew if anyone saw you act they'd see how incredibly talented you are." Phoebe was thrilled, but Griffin hardly responded. She let go of him. "When is the audition?"

Griffin looked away. "I have to call this agent tomorrow afternoon and find out."

Phoebe was confused by Griffin's edgy posture. "Aren't you excited? Griffin, it's such a wonderful opportunity."

"I know," he said, his voice full of sadness.

He leaned his head limply on her shoulder. When Phoebe brushed her face against his she felt a dampness. She kissed him lightly on the cheek and tasted salt and water. Griffin was crying.

Phoebe pulled him down until they both were kneeling on the cold grass. She held his chin and made him look at her. Gently she wiped the tears from his face.

"I don't know what to do," Griffin admitted finally, his voice shaky and weak. "I know deep inside that if I really want to be an actor I have to take this chance. I don't just mean this audition" — he hesitated — "I mean leave Rose Hill, and move to New York City for good."

Phoebe let go of him. At last she understood. Suddenly she was aware of the cold and shivered as an icy breeze shot through the thin flannel. The ground was so wet and cold it made her bare legs ache.

"When would you leave?"

"Tomorrow morning."

"What about school?"

"I can study in New York, get my diploma there."

"Where will you live?"

"This agent said I can stay at his apartment until I get settled."

"What did your mom say?"

"She left it up to me." He shook his head. "Phoebe, none of that matters. There's only one thing that's important, one thing that holds me here" — he looked at her again and took her shoulders — "and it's you."

Phoebe went limp, like a rag doll. For a

moment she was completely empty, drained, there was nothing inside her. Then in a burst of desperation she flung her arms up around Griffin's neck and pressed as close as she could. She wanted to be so close that she was part of him, so if he did go away she would always be with him.

"What should I do?" he pleaded. They finally let each other go and sat in silence.

"You should go," Phoebe heard herself say. Her voice was so dull and removed it was as though the sound had come from someone else.

"But I love you," Griffin urged, "I've never loved anyone like this before. How can I leave you?"

Phoebe smiled, but felt her own tears starting to flow. Griffin had taught her so much about living for the moment, going after what was really important in life. She had to return his gift.

"You have to grab this opportunity. It's what you want, you know it is. So you have to take it one hundred percent."

Phoebe couldn't say any more. It was impossible. Her throat had tightened up, and the harder she tried to hold back her tears the more intense the pressure became. At last she got enough control to tell Griffin the most important thing. "Griffin," she whispered, "I love you."

"I know." He nodded.

"I love you. I love you."

Griffin held her again, but this time the fierceness was gone. His touch was soft and tender, and when they kissed their tears blended together.

"I'll write," Griffin told her.

"Me too."

"I'll call."

"Yes."

"We'll still see each other."

"I know."

They stood up slowly, both covered with dirt and blades of wet grass. "Phoebe, I'm going to get that part, I know I am."

"I do too."

They were stalling and they both knew it. It was time. The decision had been made, and they had to say good bye.

"I love you," Griffin said. He started to back up but still held her hand.

"I love you," Phoebe called letting his hand slide away. He continued to back up towards the street.

Griffin stopped when he reached the sidewalk and stood for a moment under a street lamp. Phoebe felt like a camera as she watched him, she was taking a picture to keep deep inside her.

Then he turned and began walking. He was gone. The pool of light along the sidewalk was still and empty.

Phoebe stood in the backyard and wrapped her arms around herself. She couldn't stop shivering. She had never felt so cold.

Chapter
25

When Chris saw Ted's red MG pull up in front of her house early Monday morning, she couldn't help running down the front walkway to greet him.

She wanted to see him so badly, to look at his strong face again and hear his voice. Happily, she opened the car door and slid into the small, low passenger seat. Holding her stack of books against her chest, she turned and stared into Ted's face.

"Hi, sport," Ted said with a grin. He was wearing his letterman's jacket, and his hair was still wet from his morning shower. His cheeks looked ruddy, and Chris could smell his spicy aftershave. He sat there with one hand on the gearshift and gave her an embarrassed smile.

Suddenly, Chris heard herself chuckle nervously. It was like being on a first date with someone you had adored from afar for ages.

Chris felt shy and giggly and she didn't quite know what to say. Ted was so handsome, and she was so attracted to him that she almost had to look away to hide her blushes. She tried to shift her position in the seat, and her books spilled noisily onto the floor.

Her nervousness was contagious, and as she bent over to collect her books, Ted leaned across to help her. Their heads came together with a dull thud.

"Owww," they both said at the same time. Immediately, Ted let his foot slide off the clutch pedal and the car jolted forward and conked out.

There was no point in trying to act cool. Chris and Ted started to laugh, and they wrapped their arms around each other's necks in a comfortable bear hug.

"Oh, Chris," Ted whispered as he buried his face in her long hair. "Boy, have I missed you!"

"I've missed you so much," she answered. She continued to hug him, feeling the soft leather of his jacket along the side of her cheek. Neither of them was sure why, but they started to laugh again.

"Do you feel better?" Ted asked finally. He had that old mischievous smile on his face.

Chris looked down. "Yeah. I'm sorry. I must have been pretty gross when I was drunk."

"Nah, you weren't too bad. Just don't make a habit of it." Ted laughed.

"Don't worry." Chris looked into his blue eyes. They were sparkling and full of warmth. She touched his cheek.

"Thanks for taking care of me when I was sick," she whispered shyly.

"Sure."

"I guess I learned how easy it is to do something you'll regret later." She remembered how silly the whole reason for their breakup was and shook her head slowly. "Are you still benched?"

"Starting this week, I'm back in there." Ted patted his letter with affection. "I guess you just didn't want to be seen with a guy on the bench. Now that I'm back in the game, we can make up. I'll have to think about that," Ted teased.

Chris bantered, "Not so fast. Wait just a minute." She turned to Ted, giving him a playful punch on the arm. "I still want to know what's going on with you and Danielle DuClos! It certainly didn't take you long to move in there, Mr. Mason."

Ted looked shocked and then started to laugh. "Danielle DuClos! Geez, Chris, she's a freshman. What do you take me for, a cradle robber? The girl can barely tie her own shoelaces."

"That didn't seem to bother you last week," Chris accused him good-naturedly.

"Ooo," whistled Ted, "a little jealous, huh, Austin?" He poked her playfully in the ribs.

"No," Chris objected, "I just . . ." Ted's poking had changed to tickling, and it was getting more merciless by the second. "Ted, stop!" Chris panted.

"Admit it! You were jealous of Danielle DuClos! Admit it!" He tickled her as thoroughly as he could.

"No, no, no!" Chris screamed, gasping for breath.

"Yes! Yes! Admit it!"

"All right, all right, I admit it." Chris shrieked.

Ted stopped immediately and held up two fingers in a victory symbol. He cocked his head. "To tell you the truth, she's not my type. Although she is pretty cute," he kidded.

"Oh?" Chris asked, as calmly as she could.

"Well, to really tell the truth, my dad made me give her a ride to school twice because he works with her dad and their car broke down. And when you saw me at the Follies, Danielle just decided to sit next to me. So you see, there never was anything between us."

"Oh," Chris said again, this time contentedly.

Ted reached down and started the car. Before pulling away from the curb, he ran his hand along the side of Chris's face and paused for a second just to look at her. Neither of them said anything. They didn't have to. Chris leaned her head on his shoulder and closed her eyes as they began the drive to school.

"Oh, Chris . . ."

"Hmmm?"

Ted had stopped the car for a red light, and Chris lifted her head to look at him. He peered into the rearview mirror and reached up to readjust it. "I ran into Sasha at her folks' bookstore yesterday."

"Yes?"

"She wanted to warn both of us that Laurie is absolutely furious and may be out to get the two of us. Boy, Bennington's sure turned out to be a real jerk if you ask me." Ted checked over his shoulder before zipping into the next lane.

Chris sat up attentively. "Laurie's mad at me?"

"Looks that way. She wasn't very happy that we left her party early. I think she was making a play for Peter."

"What does that have to do with me?"

Ted smiled. "Peter helped rescue you. He left the party to give Phoebe a ride home. I don't think he was ever really interested in Laurie anyway, but I guess she just doesn't believe that she can't satisfy every little whim she has."

Chris remembered how Laurie had treated Brenda and felt a wave of anger. She realized now that Laurie Bennington was intolerant and mean. She should never have let Laurie get away with snubbing her sister. She should have stood up to her with more firmness.

"According to Sasha, the party pretty much broke up after we left, so the evening turned out to be a total dud for Laurie . . ."

"And she thinks it's all my fault."

"I guess so."

"Uh-oh." Chris waved to a car of kids as Ted pulled into the Kennedy parking lot. He swiftly maneuvered the small car into a space and flicked off the ignition.

"Don't worry about it. If she tries something, just ignore it. Who cares, anyway?"

Chris thought for a minute. Before, she would have cared deeply if she knew that Laurie Bennington was set on making trouble for her. But for some reason, today she found it easy to take Ted's advice. She smiled gaily.

"You're right, Ted. You're absolutely right."

"I am?" he asked, his blue eyes wide in mock innocence.

Chris didn't need to answer. She leaned forward and laced her hands around his neck. Lightly, she kissed him on the mouth. Ted pulled her in closer and kissed her again.

"Hey, Austin," he teased, "you'd better watch it. Kissing in a public place. There are rules against that kind of thing. What if everybody broke those rules? Can you imagine. . . ."

Chris laughed and realized how silly her words must have sounded before. Sometimes, rules had to be ignored, or at least bent a little. She stopped Ted's mouth with another kiss.

"I don't care, Ted Mason," she said happily, "I just don't care."

Chapter
26

Laurie looked at Peter through the thick glass of the radio station booth. She pressed the high heels of her boots into the floor and thought about how much she hated him — almost as much as she hated Chris. They would both pay for what they had done to her. It was one thing she knew for sure.

Laurie paused to think over her plan of attack. She smoothed her short hair, then, when the red "on air" light went off, she entered the control room.

"Hello Peter," she said with a smile that oozed phony sweetness. "I'm so glad to see you again. I'm here for my activities update program." She threw her leather jacket onto the control board with open hostility. Her tone was sugarcoated cyanide. There was no way Peter could miss her message.

Peter realized immediately that Laurie was

furious at him for rejecting her. Her manner was a combination of honey and venom. He decided to ignore her underlying anger and just respond to the surface saccharine. Calmly, he lifted her jacket off the board and rested it on the back of his chair. "Okay. You'll be on in five minutes. Do you remember how to work everything?" he asked politely.

Laurie glared at him. She wasn't sure how she'd wanted him to react, but distant courtesy was definitely not high on her list. She tried a different tact. "I think so, Peter. It's not very hard. A two-year-old could run this station."

"Yeah?" Peter challenged. But then he realized he'd let himself be drawn into Laurie's game. He smiled and tried to ignore her as she stood behind him and annoyingly drummed her long fingernails on the inside of the window.

After five minutes, which felt like forever, it was time for Laurie to go on the air. Peter bent over the end of the control board and motioned for her to sit in the chair. "When I flick the switch and you see the on air light go on, start talking. Ready?" He was really trying to act normal.

"Yes, Peter dear," Laurie said sarcastically as she sat down in front of the mike.

Peter shuddered and waited for the last few bars of the Bruce Springsteen song to end. As the music began to fade, he nodded to Laurie and flicked the switch.

"Hello, Cardinals," she began, "this is Laurie Bennington, a fresh, new voice on WKND."

She was trying to sound sexy and professional,

but Peter could still hear the edge of hostility in her voice.

"I'm going to be on the air twice a week, every week, to fill you in with the latest details on all the events here at Kennedy High. Now won't that be a nice change instead of the same old boring stuff every day?"

Laurie leaned into the microphone and quickly read her list of upcoming activities. For Peter, it was like listening to someone drag fingernails across a chalkboard.

Finishing reading her list, Laurie folded up the piece of paper noisily. Peter put his hands over his ears, imagining how the crinkling sound came across over the air. He waited for Laurie to sign off, but she kept talking.

"So, fellow Cardinals, that's the official news. But there's some much more interesting news just floating around. And your Laurie has decided to bring both kinds of news to you. To start with, there have been some surprising developments among a few prominent members of the junior class."

Peter stared at Laurie. He couldn't believe what she was doing. She was actually taking the liberty of turning her air time into a private gossip show. Peter was outraged. The worst part was that if anybody could get away with something like this, it was Laurie Bennington.

"First, I hear that a certain fickle redhead has dropped a big man on campus. Keep in mind, girls, that when homecoming comes around, there's one very eligible guy who may not have a date. And there's other news . . . news about a blond junior known for her academic accomplishments. Now this is a girl who has a quarterback for a boyfriend and a stepsister who, to put it mildly, is a bit of a black sheep."

Laurie was taking off now. She was dripping with vengeance.

"This blond went to a party last week. I'm sure you all heard about the big bash at the home of a certain popular junior — anyone who is anybody was there. Well, what do you think this blond honor student decided to do? It seems that she was worried that the party might not be lively enough, so she took it upon herself . . ."

Suddenly, Laurie became aware that the voice of Paul McCartney was swelling within the control room. Peter angrily turned the volume knob with a forceful twist. Laurie was completely drowned out. When she looked back down at the board, she saw that the on-air light had been turned off.

Peter turned away from the turntable and abruptly faced Laurie. He was steaming.

"All right, Laurie. I can't stop you from coming on this station, but if I ever catch you trying to ruin somebody's reputation again, there may be murder over the air waves."

Laurie stood up fiercely. "You just try it! I'm here representing the student council, and you have no right to cut me off. I'm going to be doing this show for the rest of my time at Kennedy, so, Peter, you'd just better get used to it!"

"I'll never get used to it or anything else about you. Now get out of my station!"

Peter pointed furiously to the hallway. He saw

poor Janie standing outside with a frightened look on her face.

"I've got news for you. It's not your station anymore. It's *our* station!" With that, Laurie gave a triumphant smile and grabbed her leather jacket from his chair. As she whipped out of the control booth, its sleeve flew up, slapping Peter across the face.

Afterwards Peter sat down in his swivel chair and rested his head in his hands. He should never have paid attention to Laurie Bennington in the first place. He knew she was trouble from the beginning, and he wasn't sure how it had gone this far. But there was one thing he did know, and you didn't have to be any kind of genius to figure it out. Laurie Bennington was on the warpath, and no one, *no one* at Kennedy High was safe.

"Phoebe Hall, are you there Phoebe Hall?"

Phoebe looked up to see Mr. Baylor hovering over her, a questioning look on his face and measuring stick in hand.

"Can you tell me Mr. Newton's third law of motion?"

Phoebe winced and blinked her eyes. She hadn't heard a thing the whole period. Oh, she'd been sitting in her seat and looking straight ahead. She'd seen Mr. Baylor write something on the chalkboard, but nothing registered. Now he wanted an answer.

"Well?"

Phoebe tried to say something, but she couldn't. The words wouldn't form on her tongue. Finally,

Mr. Baylor tapped Phoebe gently on the shoulder, "That's okay. That question is a toughy. Some days I'm not even sure I could answer it."

Mr. Baylor moved off down the aisle. Phoebe blinked once more. She felt a warm, wet drop forming around her eyelid. What had happened? Was she totally falling apart? Now even Mr. Baylor was letting her off the hook.

The bell rang, but Phoebe continued to stare straight ahead. Just then the tear slid down her face and plopped onto the top of her desk. Using her sleeve, Phoebe quickly rubbed it away. She clutched her books and stood up. She had to get out of there. It was lunchtime, but there was no way she was going out to the quad. She didn't want to see Woody, Sasha, Chris or anyone. She wanted to be alone. Phoebe headed out the door of science class and turned left towards the front of the school.

She found herself wandering down the main hall. She heard bits and pieces of Peter's radio show and snatches of conversation about Laurie Bennington and WKND, but she didn't even try to make sense of it. She was too tired to make sense of anything. Besides, she felt so unlike herself. The old soda pop feeling was gone now, but she felt flat, hollow, lifeless. Everything looked faded and dull. Even her tears flowed as if by reflex.

Phoebe stopped when she heard someone approaching her, but she didn't turn. Her name was being called, but the sound was so foggy and dim.

"Phoebe! Phoebe!!"

When Phoebe felt a firm hand on her arm, she finally turned. Lisa Chang was standing next to her, her dark eyes full of concern. After a quick glance down each end of the hall, Lisa took Phoebe and guided her outside.

No one else was at the main entrance. The wind was blowing hard, and the flag made a sharp snapping sound. The parking lot sretched out before them, a huge rectangle of grey. Lisa sat Phoebe down.

"Phoebe. Are you okay? What happened?"

"Hi, Lisa," Phoebe mumbled.

"What is it?"

"It's . . . everything."

Lisa looked confused. "Did something happen with Brad?"

"No. Not just Brad."

"Is it that guy you came to the rink with?"

Phoebe nodded.

"Oh, Phoebe. I knew something was up when you came to see me. It was obvious there was a lot going on between you two." She said it simply, with no harshness or judgment.

Phoebe really looked at Lisa for the first time that afternoon. Suddenly Phoebe was so glad that Lisa was there. She took a deep breath and it all came out. She told Lisa about falling in love with Griffin and breaking off with Brad. She also managed to tell Lisa about Griffin's leaving without any tears. It was almost as though she couldn't stop talking. Her old friend listened intently.

"Lisa, it really hurts. I already miss Griffin so much. I never felt like this before, so empty and alone. What am I going to do?"

Lisa thought for a moment. "Just what you usually do," she finally answered.

Phoebe looked at her friend who was so composed and strong and wished that she could run off from school to another world the way Lisa did. "You're so lucky you get to go to the rink every day. You're lucky that's all you have to think about."

Lisa smiled sadly. "You think so? I think you're the lucky one."

"Me?"

"Uh huh. I know how much you hurt right now, but I was just thinking how much I envy you."

"How can you say that?"

"Because to love somebody that much, as much as you do, that's a lot more what life is about than skating in circles by yourself in a freezing ice rink. Honest."

"C'mon."

"No, really."

Phoebe looked at Lisa and realized for the first time that there was sadness in her eyes. Maybe what Lisa was saying was true.

"I don't know," Phoebe finally admitted. "You fall in love and then it ends and other people get hurt and you just feel empty and awful. Maybe it's better to just avoid it altogether."

"If you don't know what it's like to feel empty and awful, you'll never know what it is to feel happy and full." Lisa paused. "I do know that being hurt is part of life. If you don't let yourself fall down, you never learn anything."

Phoebe remembered Griffin saying the same

275

thing. If she hadn't known Griffin she might not have figured out that Brad was the wrong person for her. And she wouldn't have figured out she had so much else inside that was waiting to be developed.

Phoebe had to admit that she did know more about herself. She understood certain feelings she could never figure out before. When she got that fizzy feeling in her stomach, she knew what it was. It was the feeling that told her she was pretending that something or someone was right for her when it really wasn't. Like with Brad. She had gone with him so long, but they really hadn't understood each other. With Griffin it had been so different. It had happened so fast, yet the connection had been deeper than with anyone she'd even known before. It was something she would never regret.

Now Lisa looked out of sorts. Phoebe leaned over to her. "Hey, you okay?"

"Sure. I was just thinking how dumb it is for me to give advice about being in love since I don't know anything about it. I probably never will."

Phoebe leaned over to her. "Don't say that. You will. Probably when you least expect it."

"This may sound weird, but I'd give anything to feel like you do right now," Lisa said wistfully.

Phoebe felt a tiny laugh burst out. The cold breeze was washing over her, but this time there was no chill, just cool clean air. "We're a great pair, aren't we?"

They both were laughing softly when a tinny

honk blasted from the entrance to the parking lot. Lisa waved to her mom who had just pulled in.

"See, off I go. I can't even stay and talk to my friends, let alone fall in love." Lisa stood up and motioned for her mom to wait.

"You were there when I needed you." Phoebe smiled. "Thanks. You really made me feel better."

"I'm glad I found you. I never get to talk about this kind of stuff, but believe me, I think about it all the time."

Lisa was backing up hesitantly. She looked as if she didn't want to leave. The horn honked again and Lisa turned sharply. She waved and ran across the parking lot.

Phoebe started to walk back toward the center of school. She moved quickly, aware that the energy had returned to her step. Her memories of Griffin and the Follies and the railroad station were there to keep. They were her own special treasures and no matter what happened, nothing could take them away from her.

When Phoebe walked out into the quad, she was glad that her other friends were still there. Chris and Ted had their arms around each other. Sasha and a few others were involved in a heated discussion about WKND. Woody was juggling three oranges and dropped them to give her a warm hug. Phoebe was feeling strong and calm. She wasn't going to explode or fade away or worry about what was going to happen. She was just going to hurt a little, that was all. With the help of her friends she'd live. As her mom used to say, the patient was alive.

She suddenly wished that she had told Lisa that love was really okay. It wasn't always easy and it wasn't always smooth, but it was definitely worthwhile.

"It's worth the effort and the pain," Phoebe thought to herself. "It really is, Lisa."

But Lisa was already heading towards the ice rink. And, as Phoebe had learned, love was something you really had to find out about on your own.

Coming soon . . .
Couples #2
Fire and Ice

Peter spun around in his chair, flicked a switch and checked a turntable. He grabbed two pairs of lightweight earphones and hung one around his neck.

"You need to wear these."

Peter leaned toward her. Lisa started to take the earphones from him, but instead he moved closer and put them over her ears himself. His face was very close to hers. Again he stopped and stared at her with the strangest, searching look. Lisa wasn't sure what it meant, but it made her feel flushed and breathless.

Peter backed away, cleared his throat, then spun around again to take out a record. Finally he flipped on the microphone with one graceful motion.

"Hello, Cardinals. This is Peter Lacey, your man at WKND here with another day of homecoming specials. This week I've been interviewing the candidates for junior princess. Today we have Lisa Chang. Hello Lisa," Peter looked at Lisa to let her know it was her turn to talk.

Lisa took a deep breath and prepared herself.

Join the Team!

They're talented. They're fabulous-looking. They're winners! And they've got what you want! Don't miss any of these exciting CHEERLEADERS books!

Watch for these titles! $2.25 each

- ☐ QI 33402-6 **Trying Out** *Caroline B. Cooney*
- ☐ QI 33403-4 **Getting Even** *Christopher Pike*
- ☐ QI 33404-2 **Rumors** *Caroline B. Cooney*
- ☐ QI 33405-0 **Feuding** *Lisa Norby*
- ☐ QI 33406-9 **All the Way** *Caroline B. Cooney*
- ☐ QI 33407-7 **Splitting** *Jennifer Sarasin*

WILDFIRE®

Move from one breathtaking love story to another with the Hottest Teen Romances in town!

NEW WILDFIRES! $2.25 each

☐ UH33328-3   **LOVING THAT O'CONNOR BOY** Diane Hoh

☐ UH33180-9   **SENIOR DREAMS CAN COME TRUE**
Jane Claypool Miner

☐ UH33268-6   **LOVE SIGNS** M.L. Kennedy

☐ UH33266-X   **MY SUMMER LOVE** Elisabeth Ogilvie

BEST-SELLING WILDFIRES!

☐ UH32890-5   **THE BOY NEXT DOOR** Vicky Martin $2.25

☐ UH33265-1   **OUT OF BOUNDS** Eileen Hehl $2.25

☐ UH33097-7   **CHRISTY'S SENIOR YEAR** Maud Johnson $2.25

☐ UH32284-2   **ANGEL** Helen Cavanagh $2.25

☐ UH32542-6   **MISS PERFECT** Jill Ross Klevin $1.95

☐ UH32431-4   **LOVE GAMES** Deborah Aydt $1.95

☐ UH32536-1   **KISS AND TELL** Helen Cavanagh $2.25

☐ UH31931-0   **SENIOR CLASS** Jane Claypool Miner $1.95

☐ UH33096-9   **CHRISTY'S LOVE** Maud Johnson $2.25

☐ UH32846-8   **NICE GIRLS DON'T** Caroline B. Cooney $2.25

Scholastic Inc.,
P.O. Box 7502, 2932 E. McCarty St., Jefferson City, MO 65102

Please send me the books I have checked above. I am enclosing
$_____ (please add $1.00 to cover shipping and handling).
Send check or money order–no cash or C.O.D.'s please.

Name _____

Address _____

City_____ State/Zip _____

Please allow four to six weeks for delivery.

WDF 852